ABJECTIFICATION

Stories & Truths

"*Abjectification* resides somewhere between #METOO and #ICONCUR, a modern macrocosm where female characters mutate from animals and changelings to 'reverse-ghost-women' who 'bleed for days but never die,' eluding, sometimes even mocking, the logic of men's worlds. This story collection both excites and paralyzes the libido."

    — Laura Jean Baker, author of *The Motherhood Affidavits: A Memoir*

"The stories in *Abjectification* are incisive and accomplished. They hang in orbit around a feeling of dread and anxiety that builds and builds with each page, each sentence, and each carefully rendered image. This is a remarkable book. I urge you to read it."

    —Kevin Powers, critically-acclaimed author of *A Shout in the Ruins* and *The Yellow Birds*

ABJECTIFICATION

Stories & Truths

C. Kubasta

Apprentice
House Press
Loyola University Maryland

The following is a work of fiction. Any resemblances to people or places are purely coincidental.

First Edition

Casebound ISBN: 978-1-62720-275-6
Paperback ISBN: 978-1-62720-276-3
Ebook ISBN: 978-1-62720-277-0

Printed in the United States of America

Design by Elisa Jonas
Promotion plan by Taylor Dacosta
Editorial development by Sofia Barr
Cover photo of model used with permission by Atelieri O. Haapala

Apprentice House Press
Loyola University Maryland
4501 N. Charles Street
Baltimore, MD 21210
410.617.5265
www.ApprenticeHouse.com
info@ApprenticeHouse.com

Books by C. Kubasta

This Business of the Flesh (Apprentice House)
Girling (Brain Mill Press)
Of Covenants (Whitepoint Press)
All Beautiful & Useless (BlazeVox)

With love for Jen & Jennifer – both of whom (in a moment of kindness) allowed me to call them Jenny

Contents

PRIMARY EMBODIMENTS

"Looking at, and listening to, these bodily ecstasies, we can also notice something else that these genres seem to share: though quite differently gendered with respect to their targeted audiences, with pornography aimed, presumably, at active men and melodramatic weepies aimed, presumably, at passive women, and with contemporary gross-out horror aimed at adolescents careening wildly between the two masculine and feminine poles, in each of these genres the bodies of women figured on the screen have functioned traditionally as the PRIMARY EMBODIMENTS of pleasure, fear, and pain."

Linda Williams
Film Bodies: Gender, Genre, and Excess

Morning After

You wake with panic in your mouth. Tangible, it fills the space between your tongue and the ridged roof of your mouth, pressing against your palate, fitting behind your teeth and stretching back to glottis.

You hold it for a moment, then realize it's both insubstantial and with form. This realization makes you bolt, and you hit your head on the metal bed frame.

Maybe you are a child again, playing hide-and-seek. (You were always good at hide-and-seek. There were times you fell asleep in hiding places and woke, disoriented. Maybe this is one of those times.)

But the throb radiating from your head calls your hands up to the source of the pain, and your hands are a woman's, not a girl's. The body you see in the dimmed light is a woman's body, not a girl's.

With you under the bed are normal things: dented cardboard boxes laced with cobwebs, accumulated gatherings of hair and dust. Spare socks missing their partners.

Blocks of dim sunlight breach the border where the blankets and sheets hang off the mattress. The floor is wooden, with glossed spots where feet have walked in and out of the room.

The door is open. You can see a hallway beyond, and how the room is bare except for the bed, and the stored items beneath it. You are one of those stored items, it seems. You still don't know where you are. Your tongue uncomfortable in your mouth.

You hear noises beyond the hallway – what sounds like a door opening, something being dragged. You shrink into yourself, as much as possible, in this space you still don't understand. Something hitting something, dragging.

A shadow approaches the open space of the door, and in the limited view afforded between the bedclothes and the floor appear booted feet.

They stop, reposition, continue.

You breathe – if what you are doing can be called breathing. You look up just in time to see what looks like yourself being dragged past the open door. That you is wearing what you are wearing. You look like yourself, but damaged, undone. Darkened blood here and there. You look down at the self under the bed, and see that what you are wearing now is rumpled but clean; your skin not marked by any abrasions. You turn back in time to see your face pass by, eyes closed, hollows blued.

Your mind splits – your mind screams at you. That's not you out the door, that's some other thing, some object.

From the hallway, you hear a swing and creak, the unoiled metal of a hinge, then a rhythmic thunk. Bone-wrapped-in-skin meeting stairs, one tread at a time.

Your tongue expands in your mouth.

•

Out from the bed, down the hall, out the door, and it's daylight, it's fall, it's leaf-crumple piles beneath your feet as your knees rise up and down and you're fast away from the house and the glossed wood floors and the sound of it hitting the stairs.

You don't know how long you've been running but your heart is fire in your chest and your lungs ragged.

You've been running in one direction, but you've never crossed a road, or a path, or seen another house. There are only blackened tree trunks and bare limbs.

You keep running and see the moon's rising, its pale echo – almost translucent – while the sun is still low in the sky.

The sky is so beautiful. If you weren't seeing it yourself, you'd think it was fake – a photo-shopped image, or tinted postcard, or movie set. The risen moon is an almost-perfect communion wafer, its edges slightly rumpled, the kind your stuttering priest might hold up for the congregation and sing, and when he sings all stutter disappears and even when you were little you knew that was a holy moment: the host and the music of a voice made perfect. The sky pinks as the sun goes down and the blaze of the sun dying underlights the edges of the clouds, making the sky impossibly more beautiful, ridges of golden light, lacings of foil and leaf, and still you're running and not getting anywhere. You can't stop looking at the sky. You look up and then look down, careful not to trip on any fallen logs or hidden rocks waiting beneath the piles of leaves in the woods silent except for your fast-patterned breathing. You know if you don't make it out of the woods you'll never make it out. You know if you stop running you'll become that thing being dragged, that spoil. You know that the noise you make running is giving you away. Nightfall; only the gibbous moon will be visible but someone with boots will come looking.

Freak Show

The first time he saw her naked he wasn't sure she was. The lighting was dim, and he thought he'd heard her taking things off – the rustle of fabric, a zipper from her jeans, but when she walked toward him in the half-light, it looked like she was still wearing something. Panties and a tank top maybe, something covering those parts of her body? The light peeking around the edges of the blinds caught at her, sharply defining her nipples, and what seemed to be just her between her legs. He reached out and touched her and it was all skin.

After, he'd flicked on the light, seen it was a tattoo – or a bunch of tattoos in the shape of a corset maybe (he thought that was what it was called) – the blue-black of ink in intricate pattern. He'd meant to get up and go to the bathroom, and clean himself up, but was held there, mesmerized. They were both catching their breaths, and he turned the light up a little more, forgetting for a minute that this was their first time together, and the bedside table's bulb might cast a harsh glare, that maybe she wouldn't want him staring. But she sat up a little, held still. As her chest rose and fell with her breathing, he traced the line that cut across her breasts, just above her nipples. It was a kind of geometric lace all down the front and sides of her breasts, then a series of intersecting lines, like crosshatching on her stomach and sides. Lines crossed the puckered skin of nipple, half obscuring areolas. He stopped and looked at her face, saw her smiling.

"Go ahead," she said, so he kept exploring. It was like a mimic of underwear, some extra layer underneath everything. He'd never seen anything like it, and never expected to see it on her.

With her clothes on, Meghan looked like the last person who would have a tattoo, let alone a full-body tattoo. She wore jeans, and button-down shirts, had shoulder-length dirty blonde hair, and barely wore any makeup. Jeff had known her family since they were both kids, when his and her parents went to the same church. They'd just run into each other again a few months ago. He newly divorced; she still single, and they'd started renewing their friendship and working up to something else. When she'd leaned over to climb up in his truck tonight and he'd caught a peek of her bra between the buttons of her shirt, he'd worked to physically calm himself, thinking he might actually get to touch her breasts – something of a dream since long-ago church suppers and awkward adolescence longing. But now, with the fluorescent bulb picking up the slivers of her skin between the patterns of deep-sunk color, he closed his eyes and ran his fingertips over the demarcation between untouched and tattooed skin, thinking he should be able to feel the difference. If he had to describe Meghan's skin, he'd have called it 'alabaster' – like certain religious statues that were white with a bluish undertone. The tattooed skin looked like flat black, like someone's hot rod paintjob in their back shed.

He was acutely aware that he was still wearing socks.

•

Her back was a labyrinth of biblical scenes: the garden and snakes and depictions of Eve and Lilith and Ruth and Naomi and Sarah and Hannah and Tamar and a whole bunch more whose stories he couldn't remember. But she could; she did. He'd trace a vining shape and slow and stop and ask her about it and she'd tell the story, still able to recite from memory and often tell the numbers of book and verse. She'd always been more attentive in classes – he remembered that. She'd go right from school to fellowship, always volunteering to help with the younger kids, staying after to clean up in the kitchen; usher for the service, plan and promote and assist with summer bible camp. He remembered how she'd been one of the good girls, selected for honors like readings during service, and scholarships from the congregation for college.

She told him she'd dated some guy in college who had a stupid tattoo, some cartoon character in multiple images around his belly, and he'd take off his shirt and spin around, like a human flipbook. She laughed when she told the story, joking about how high he must have been when he had the idea, when he'd do the performance, maybe even when he got the tattoo. But she said he'd been sweet, if stupid, and taken her to get her first one.

"Which one?" Jeff had asked. He couldn't even see a 'one' – a single piece that was separate from the rest of

them, tangled around her, enclosing her body. Since they'd
been dating for a few months, he'd had more time to look,
and noticed how she wasn't entirely covered – her back
piece greyed out just past the downward curve of her ass.
On the front, the linear sidepieces softened into a floral
motif at her hipbones and blended into her bush. All sorts
of flowers – large blooms and small, violets & hibiscus &
hydrangea & spirea & various kinds of orchids with their
well-articulated pistils and stamen.

She laughed. "It's covered now – it was stupid. A turtle,
in color," she wrinkled her nose. All her work was black
lines of various thicknesses, some shading in grey. But no
color, anywhere, even in the florals and vines. She didn't
like color, she said, the way it looked on her skin. Jeff tried
to think what he was doing then: when Meghan was dating
some guy who liked to take off his shirt and spin around
to make his cartoon tattoo come alive. Maybe he and his
wife were up nights with the baby, starting to spin apart.
No sleep, no sex, wondering what they had in common
or why they got married. When their baby girl died, all of
the sudden with no one to blame, they'd each flung free of
everything they'd been holding onto. By the time Meghan
would decide she didn't like the tattoo and begin the long
process of covering the skin that was almost always covered
anyway, Jeff would have done some terrible things to cover
the guilt he felt about abandoning his wife when she needed
him most. He'd asked Meghan where that first tattoo had
been, and she'd touched low on her back, somewhere near
the figure of Sarah.

•

Meghan would disappear sometimes, for a few weeks, claiming she was busy with work, but he figured out that it was because she was having some new work done – a large piece – and didn't want to be touched or bothered during the healing. She'd return after the scabbing was done, the greyed feathering of ink and skin that shed when it was touched, and she'd returned to her regular smoothness, with a new design patterning down the long planes of her thighs, or circling her biceps or forearms. Sometimes these multi-step processes occurred over several months, and each grew until they touched one other, filling in the spaces of cream skin. Each time she showed him something new it was like the reveal of the first night; he'd never know what it would be because it was hidden beneath full-sleeved shirts and long pants, and then when she'd disrobe there'd be some-thing new to absorb the light. He became attuned to the subtle variation of brand-new versus slightly-aged tattoos, the way even black ink was slightly blued, but on her they all started to seem like shades of Vantablack, absorbing more light than seemed natural – some trick of the lab, a black hole of chaos embedded in her skin. He'd read about Vantablack somewhere, that it held the world's record for the darkest man-made substance, absorbing even more than visible light. Coated with it, three-dimensional objects appeared two-dimensional. Meghan's body being remade seemed to absorb all light too – even in a pitch-black room, she was its darkest center. Sometimes he thought he was disappearing into her; sometimes he thought he wanted to disappear into her the way they fucked, he'd go harder and harder, only stopping when she put her ghost-white hand on his chest and pushed back.

After he and his wife lost their little girl, the middle-of-the-night baby monitor gone quiet and her infant body already cold when he went to check on her as he was pacing the house around 5 AM, their house had become a black hole, but it hadn't been much more than that even before. They'd married when she got pregnant, months before either of them would have ever thought of it on their own. At the wedding, each of the professionally-taken photos revealed his pinched smiles, and the way she tried to not rest her hands on her belly, to keep the secret until after the ceremony as much as they could. Their parents knew, of course, and had been eager to go all in for the wedding, as long as there was a wedding. Whether or not the bride and groom were really in love, or really ready, hadn't been anyone's concern. The baby on the way made it so – God had spoken. So when Jeff had lifted his daughter out of the bassinet tucked inside the crib she'd never grow into, and felt her heaviness, the way she had already cooled, he wondered immediately, before he could stop himself, if God had spoken again. Maybe God had been speaking all along, in the quiet spaces of the house laced with resentment since she'd been born, in the ways his wife rolled over and sighed heavily whenever he tried to touch her, in the metallic sound of the sofa pullout that he made into his bed most nights in the living room.

But he didn't have anyone to blame, God or otherwise, for what he'd done after that. Sure, he hadn't been prepared for the kind of grief and guilt and anger and shame that settled on him in the intervening days after their little girl died. But when he held her that first morning, and knew she was gone, he could have made a different decision. What he decided was to put her back in her crib, and leave early for work so that his wife would find her and have to deal with it alone. And when he'd got the call and come back home, he never came clean that he was anything but caught-out and devastated. He walked back into his house, all pretended surprise and world-come-crashing-down and accepted being held and the love of his mother and mother-in-law and never told any of them that he'd orchestrated that moment, to save himself and leave his poor kid-of-a-wife adrift on her own. A few days later, he accepted his wife's sister holding him, and that had been his doing too.

He was fine with Meghan disappearing when she needed to. Better that than anything that would remind him of his wife — the thought that if he went to touch her, any part of her, and she moved away, or stopped him, or sighed, he'd be brought back, through the telescoping of time, to when that was the usual response to his hands, his mouth.

After they'd been dating about a year and a half, they went to Chicago for a weekend to a big exhibit at one of the museums on the history of tattooing. They watched videos of traditional methods, people marked by instruments made of sticks, or pins, or soot pressed into skin on quills. Meghan would pause in front of the screens, studying elders working with rudimentary implements, but Jeff couldn't watch for long, after seeing the person-being-tattooed faces' wincing,

15

pale with pain. There were silicone molds of body parts that had been worked on by artists in their signature styles; Meghan would go beyond what was written on the museum plaque, pointing and explaining what she liked about each style, spending time with the life-sized legs and torsos like they were landscapes or portraits in an art museum. Once, Jeff reached out to touch one of the torsos, and a guard stopped him. Meghan was partial to the Yakuza style; Jeff recognized the dense patterning of the black figures that was working its way down the back of her thigh.

There was a live demonstration, a man on a padded table. First, his chest was shaved, and then the tattoo artist started creating a large design near the top of his abdomen, following the lines of a stencil. Jeff watched for a long time, because the man didn't seem bothered by the pain. He was a little flushed, but seemed more excited – the tattoo gun buzzed in the artist's glove-wrapped hand. He stood watching, trying to imagine if this was part of the experience that Meghan enjoyed, but when he turned to ask her, she was gone. She was watching a video about American Jews who were getting replicas of the tattoos forced on their grandparents during the Holocaust. In the video, the grandchildren were sitting next to their grandparents, if they were alive, or holding photographs of them, if they weren't.

At dinner that night, Jeff asked Meghan if she'd want to get a tattoo with him.

"You're not suggesting we get something *together*?" She took a big gulp of her drink, and looked nervous. "Like a couples-tattoo?"

"No," he laughed. He was definitely not suggesting that. "I just meant I was thinking of getting something, something small. And it might be kind of hot to get them at the same time."

"Like, instead of a couples massage, we're just on side-by-side tables?"

"Yeah, like that."

"Don't take this the wrong way, Jeff – but no."

He didn't take it the wrong way, not really. He wasn't sure he wanted one anyway. He worried he'd look like a wimp next to her. Or that he couldn't handle her on the table, laid out like that, and then continue on. But he felt like they had to – in some way – talk about it, or at least the idea of it, and about the exhibit. Thank god she said no.

They were in the hotel bed that night, naked, slightly-sweaty, splayed out on the clean white sheets they'd never have to wash, when Meghan said, "If you want a tattoo, you should get one – I didn't mean to discourage you. I just like being alone for mine – it's not something I want to share."

He took her hand, pale cream against the white sheets, "It's OK – I don't really want one." His body, covered in a layer of soft brown hair, read as grey tones against the bleached sheen of the bedding. Meghan created some kind of optical illusion, disappearing, but for her hands and feet, her unmarked shoulders, neck and face. Her left leg was still undone below the knee, and some of her right, beginning around the shin bone seemed to swim up from the darkness that was the rest of her. She turned her head toward him and smiled.

"I wondered."

She kept her head turned, looking at him.

"How much does it hurt?"

She laughed. "Not much," she turned her head so she was looking up at the ceiling. "Depends where, depends on how long it takes. Skin gets more sensitive after a while, if it takes more than a few hours." She was still lacing her fingers through his, and went on to mention the difference between bone, muscle, certain areas of fat like her ass, the soft sides of stomach. She told him about sitting in the waiting area, and some dudebro trying to chat her up, thinking she might be nervous, that it was her first time, that she was there for some cute butterfly, or maybe an inspirational quote.

Jeff had never been into a tattoo shop, let alone hers, but he'd driven past it a bunch of times, slowed down and looked into the windows. He could picture the dark leather couches, the private rooms beyond. He could picture her sitting there waiting, fully covered, maybe in a ribbed turtleneck sweater, or long-sleeved t-shirt that hid everything. And he could see the kind of guy she was talking about now – in short sleeves with tribal tattoos and barbwire wrapping his biceps and forearms – scoping her out and reassuring her about her appointment. Meghan said she and the artist had a good laugh at that. The artist, the only one she went to now, who did all the designs and all her work, later told her he'd cried during his back piece and tried to say it was allergies. She'd said men cry more than women anyway, but always try to pretend they're the tough ones.

That reminded Jeff of something his dad had told him once: You can't trust a woman because she'll bleed for days but never die. Jeff had been young, eleven or twelve, and had not understood what he meant. Maybe it was a joke. After he went home that day, his house full of women – his wife, his mother, mother-in-law, sister-in-law – he'd thought of that again. The hole that had been torn in their world by the dying of their daughter was being closed by those women, and he had no place in it: the healing, or the new world. Maybe what he'd done with his wife's sister was some kind of attempt to re-make the hole and fit himself back in. In that moment, he understood that what his father was saying was that he was afraid of women and that Jeff should be too.

•

Meghan went home to see her family every few months; Jeff tried not to ask her too much about it. Mostly *Did you have a good weekend? How's everyone doing?* After one of those visits and their stilted conversations, she said, "I know Jeff."

"Know what?"

"Your parents and my parents are still friends."

"Oh."

"It's a small town, you know." Jeff could imagine what her parents thought of him, what everyone thought of him. His ex-wife still lived there, his ex-family, his ex-sister-in-law, and he wasn't stupid enough to think the stories of what he'd done would have been kept quiet. His ex-wife and ex-sister-in-law had made up, decided (with his ex-mother-in-law's help) that he was the problem after all. They'd sliced him from their lives cleanly with the divorce papers. He'd made it easier by moving away, and kept his distance. He figured if his mother ever wanted to talk to him again, she knew where he was, but until then he'd just stay gone so they could make whatever devil of him they wanted.

"Do they know we're dating?"

"I haven't told them," Meghan was setting the table in her small apartment, finishing the dinner she'd made for them.

"You must think I'm a terrible person." He stood up from the chair he'd been sitting in, started to put on his coat.

"Jeff." She was holding a steaming sauce pan of pasta and sauce, her hands shielded with hot pads. "I've always known what happened."

"Oh." He sat back down, "Always? Since before we started dating?"

"Yup."

"And you still . . .?" She set the pot down on the hot pad waiting in the center of the table, then took the chair across from him. He put his coat back on his chair and sat back down but didn't relax. She took off the hot pads, one at a time, holding eye contact with him.

"I don't know what it's like to lose a child – what that does to a person. That's not something I would be able to understand. I –" she paused, stirring what was in the pot. "I'm not going to judge you for what you did."

They sat and ate most of the meal in silence. Pasta was about all Meghan knew how to make. Sometimes it was with red sauce, sometimes olive oil and herbs with parmesan on top, but he liked it best when she made a cream sauce. Red sauce kept him up at night with heartburn. As they were washing the dishes, her hands in the soapy water, and him standing next to her, taking plates and pots and silverware from the dry rack, running the towel over them and putting them away, she said, "When I talk to God, I ask for understanding most of the time. My parents' church usually pisses me off. There are a lot of people there who seem really sure they know what God thinks – about sin, and love, and hell, and forgiveness. But mostly I think it's what they think."

She passed him a glass, and he took it carefully and dried the outside and inside, set it upside down in the cupboard.

"If my parents knew about my tattoos, they'd think I was sinning, going to hell – but I'm not hurting anyone, so I don't think God minds."

Jeff was awake all night, his stomach churning. He got up a couple times to drink milk straight out of the carton, but it didn't help. He didn't know what exactly Meghan knew about him – what he'd done to his family – and he wasn't going to ask. He should've known she'd probably heard things about him and had been keeping that inside for almost three years now. More than all that, he couldn't imagine her sitting in that church, probably seeing his ex-wife, maybe her sister. Maybe it was like lying on a tattoo table, breathing through the pain, feeling every bit of it and coming out the other side. She'd once told him she found a long tattoo appointment like meditation. But what really bothered him was that she believed in God, that she talked to God. He didn't really know her at all.

•

That summer, they decided to rent a cabin for a weekend, and went with another couple, Chuck and Lacey. They'd gotten together for drinks and darts once a week or so, and sometimes for dinner, or to go bowling. Chuck and Lacey had gotten married a few years ago, and Jeff and Meghan went to the wedding. They'd had fun, dressing up fancy and dancing, but agreed that they were happy with things as they were. Meghan let Jeff know she had no desire to ever get married or have kids. Jeff had been relieved.

They'd found a cabin on a website and picked it because it came with a pontoon boat, and was remote from any other properties. Meghan was a little nervous about being uncovered – even in the summer she'd wear long pants and full sleeves unless they were at one of their places, or in bed. But at the wedding, Lacey had looked beautiful in a sleeveless dress that showed off all her work, and Chuck had his own tattoos, fading old ones where the once-letters had blurred to unreadability.

The first night they arrived late, grilled steaks, and stayed up late playing Rummy, drinking themselves into a fuzzy mid-morning start the next day, until the lake called to them, all cloudless blue sky and early heat.

Meghan wore a high-necked one-piece with a skirted bottom. When she stepped on the deck with her tote and towel, Lacey gasped. Chuck let out a friendly whistle and nudged Jeff, saying something like he *never would have guessed*. They cruised the series of interlocking lakes from late morn-ing to late afternoon, slipping beers out of the ice-packed cooler, commenting on the patches of woods and lake houses. Meghan reapplied a high-SPF formula sunscreen that matched the shade of her unmarked skin, liberally and often. Jeff and Chuck and Meghan tried to keep conversation going, but every time they looked at Lacey her face was pinched and red.

That night dinner was tense. In their room, Jeff and Meghan could hear the other two arguing late into the night. Lacey accused Chuck of all sorts of things, mostly leering at Meghan, wanting her, and then they both heard her crying. They tried to stay in their room later on Sunday, and when they ventured out, there was a full pot of coffee and a note: *Thanks for the weekend! We decided to get an early start – see you soon, Lacey & Chuck.* Meghan looked at Jeff as she poured his cup, her eyebrows raised.

"I don't think we'll be seeing them soon," she said. "They think I'm a freak show."

Jeff led her back to the bedroom, unbelted her robe and kissed every inch of her, the charcoal-blue patterns, the untouched places of her hands and feet and neck, the slightly pink swells on the top of her breasts, because no matter how many times she applied sunscreen, she was sensitive to exposure.

•

That fall, it had been a month – longer it seemed – since he'd seen her, and when it came, the reveal, he couldn't figure out what was new. Maybe some touch-up, but she usually didn't go into hiding unless it was a large piece that needed time and space to heal. By now, she was done; or looked done to him. The top line was as when he'd first seen her – a hard line across the top of her breasts, like a Victorian corset, but the shoulders bare; full arm sleeves; torso; leg work that stopped just above the rounded knob of the ankle. She was a reverse-ghost-woman: only her hands and feet and face untouched by the needle.

In bed, watching his hands move across her, disappearing in and out of the palimpsest of her, he still didn't notice anything new. But when she was on top, he wove his hands into her hair – the same as always, dark blonde and shoulder-length, blunt cut – and felt something new, underneath the weight of it, along the hairline, a bristle of newly growing hair. He twisted his hands into fists, pulled fast, waited until she came and collapsed onto him, until her breathing slowed.

"Can I see it?"

She rolled over and switched on the light.

He could barely see it through the new hair that was growing out, growing through it.

"I thought your place wouldn't do neck or face . . ." he drew it out, a half question, already afraid of the answer.

"She made an exception."

"I can't see it," he put on his glasses, squinted as he held her hair up and out of the way.

"You're not meant to," she said quickly, pulling away from him.

"*I'm* not meant to – or *no one* is meant to?"

"Whichever."

He didn't understand. Why get a tattoo under hair, where she won't ever see it? What was it? She'd never

24

moved away like that before. Usually this looking – especially after she got a new one – was part of their ritual:
disappear, return, sex, show it off. He knew there was something about the way she was always covered, concealed,
that made the revealing special, something more intimate
between the two of them. He knew that since the weekend with Chuck and Lacey she wasn't interested in anyone
else seeing her. She'd become even more careful about her
clothes, buttoning every button, checking every seam. But
if she was getting work she didn't want him to see, then he
was a part of the anyone else.

But more than that, he felt different suddenly. When
she started to move on him, shifting her hips faster, as
they both got closer, he'd reached up and felt the bristled
hair and flashed back to Lacey's face on the boat: disgust.
He'd worked to get her off then, knowing he couldn't finish. When they'd overheard Chuck and Lacey arguing,
he'd understood that Lacey was just lobbing bombs, creating a diversion. She didn't really think Chuck was into
Meghan, but she couldn't say what she really thought. *There
is something wrong with that woman.* Flat on his back now, her
on top, his mind skirted the edge of something: Meghan's
face loomed up out of the darkness she'd made of her own
body, and that body had swallowed him. Right now, at this
moment, it was holding onto him, claiming some part of
him and he started to panic that he'd never be able to get
it back. Jeff thought back to how Meghan had known all
along what he'd done, how after coming home to his baby
dead he'd gone to his wife's sister's bed and fucked her, and
somehow her response had been, *I'll take him.* He thought

maybe she just liked pain after all, maybe she liked lying on that padded table and letting that woman tattoo artist sink a needle all over her body. Her skin that should be staying soft and untouched was becoming armor, scar tissue he wasn't allowed to see. Her skull would be one of those places that really hurt, bone just under a sheathing of skin.

But mostly he knew that his dad had been right: you couldn't trust them.

How It Was for Him

Hal met her at the local bar, out with his friend Russ. Russ and a girl named Emma paired off, and Hal ended up talking to Emma's roommate, who went by the name Les, but he wasn't sure if that was her first name, or her last, or short for something or a nickname. They'd ended up back at the girls' room. Right away, Hal noticed the difference between his dorm room and theirs: it was much bigger, with high ceilings and wooden floors. They went to the local girls' school – Les had corrected him, "women's college" (with a wink). The dorms were shabby, old buildings, but large. Stately almost.

Hal and Russ went to the state school a few towns over. They shared a quad with two other guys, and their room was maybe a third of the girls' – women's – rooms here. Their bunk beds were stacked tight against the walls and there wasn't room for desks or any other furniture. Also, they were guys – so he couldn't imagine doing half of the things these girls had, almost-curtains, and candles, and little things everywhere that seemed to match. Emma and Les each had a single bed, a desk, a dresser, and a big wardrobe; they'd split the room in half and each had their own space. The way they set up their wardrobes it was like two separate rooms, with a hallway between them. And, maybe because they were *women* (he was trying really hard to remember to say that) they had sheets that matched their blankets, or that's what it looked like.

Hal knew what was going to happen when they went back to their room, but still, they moved pretty fast. First, Emma grabbed them all beers from the mini-fridge, and they talked a little, but soon all Hal could see was the bottom of Russ's socked feet and the beginnings of his legs all tangled up on Emma's bed, so he wasn't surprised when Les took his hand and led him over to hers. It's why he and Russ had gone out in the first place – Fall Break, and a Wednesday night, and neither of them quite ready to drive the next forty-five minutes home. Home was still two lakes over, the little town they'd just barely escaped two months before. They'd heard the girls here were a little wild and that the local bar didn't card often. Besides, it's not like their families were expecting them. Hal's dad didn't keep in touch, and Russ's brother had stayed at home working. Both of them being the first to go to college meant their families didn't really know about things like fall break, or that they had an extra-long weekend this time in October.

Les pushed him down on the bed and climbed on top, straddling his hips. She smiled a slightly drunken smile and reached down to the hem of her shirt, pulling it off over her head. She was wearing a fancy bra that pushed her tits up and together. As his eyes wandered from the lacy edge, he noticed the dark hair in her armpits and started. *She doesn't shave.* It was a fully-formed sentence in his head. Hal had never seen a woman with armpit hair before – the incongruity of the girly bra and the straight dark hair that shadowed under her arms made him sit up a little, as a small audible exhalation escaped his mouth. He reached out, but instead of touching the curved flesh in her bra, he reached for her pits, took a little of the hair between two of his fingers, sort of petted it. Les laughed.

"What?" she asked, "Haven't you seen armpit hair before?"

"Not on a girl," he said. He could hear himself slurring a little.

"Got a problem with it?"

"No."

"Good," she laughed again, sliding her hands down his legs. He could hear Les laughing again, and she was down by his feet, working on one of the double knots he tied on his laces. He hated when his laces came untied, so always double-knotted them, something Russ made fun of him for. He was wearing a cheap pair of hiking boots, with the red and orange cord laces, and he'd knotted them extra tight tonight. Les had one of his boots off and was tugging on his sock. Gross. He slid to the end of the bed and undid his other boot and sock himself. He laid back down, then arched up a little, helping her to slide his jeans off under him, his boxers. He sat up then and took his own shirt off, only embarrassed for a minute about his belly. It was pale, even in the dim dorm room light, and he could tell he'd already begun gaining weight – the Freshman Fifteen everyone talked about. His grandmother, his mother's mother, had always called him "zaftig." He looked it up once, so he knew what it meant.

He kissed her then. If they were going to have sex, he thought they should at least do some kissing first. It was a little sloppy, both of them beery-tasting, and wobbly from the shots at the bar, but it was good.

Russ. Was he really going to fuck in the same room as his best friend? Was Russ doing that right now? Russ had known Emma before tonight. She was a local girl, and somehow she knew his twin brother. Maybe they'd partied together in high school, their towns only a few counties apart, and all the places around so small and spread thin. Most of the schools funneled their resources for team sports, or clubs, or anything else where a certain number of bodies were needed. Maybe Hal had met Emma before too, but he didn't think so. He didn't remember her face.

Les seemed to like to lay on top of him, resting all her weight across his chest. He could feel the scratchiness of that bra, and where the wires were, but also how she was shorter and smaller. But where she laid on him she made a warm spot, a shadow of heat on top of the covers of her dorm room bed. She kissed aggressively too – tongue, but then using her teeth to take little nipping bites, pressing down with all her force. After a little bit, he relaxed into the pillow and let her do the work. She slid her face down the sides of his face, into his neck, biting still, leaving him with a warm wet feeling ringing all around his face as he breathed into the air above him. His hands circled from her back to her shoulders to her tits, until he could figure out how to unhook her bra.

She surprised him though when she moved quick to his nipple, and bit it kind of hard. He jerked and half sat up.

"Oh – too much?"

He only nodded at first, but found his voice. "Yeah," he whispered, "that hurt."

"Sorry," she said, although she didn't sound sorry. She went back to his nipple but this time only used her tongue, circling it a little, keeping her teeth mostly to herself. He stayed tensed. He didn't think he'd had his nipples done like that before. He wasn't sure if he liked it or not. From across the room, he heard some whispers and rustling and turned his head toward the sounds. But these girls had it figured out. A desk was backed up against the long-side of the bed, blocking the view of the other side of the room. He couldn't have seen anything, even if he'd wanted to. This wasn't the first time they'd done the doubles thing.

Les was working her way down his belly, and now he really tensed, hyper aware of trying to suck in his gut, hoping that laying down made it look smaller, hoping she wouldn't think he was fat. She wasn't exactly skinny, but smaller than him in every way, and besides, after seeing those tits and that bra, he wasn't really looking at whether she had a flat belly. He thought the armpits were going to be the biggest surprise of the night, but then she took him in her mouth.

It wasn't that Hal hadn't gotten head before. He had, but it had always been quick, part of the lead-up to sex. His girlfriend from high school didn't really seem to like it, so it was only once in a while, and then just for a few seconds to get him lubed up for what came after. This felt different, right away. If he really thought about it, he never knew what the big deal was about blow jobs anyway. It always just felt like sticking it in a bowl of warm water. It was nice, kind of comforting, but he liked a hand better, and better than that he like to have sex. He'd only been with three girls really: his girlfriend, and two college hookups. The hookups were fine, but it's not like they were anything more than that. His girlfriend he'd loved (or thought he did) so what he'd really wanted to do was *be* with her, and then after to lay with her, and that was something they didn't get to do very often – what with both of their work schedules, and her parents, and if they went to his house, his brother or sister would always be around the house.

But now Les was swirling her tongue around his dick, and at the same time, she seemed to have a hand on his dick, maybe turning it in the opposite direction, and it didn't feel comforting at all. It felt like he might be about to come.

He did. Goddamn it, he did. He came in her mouth. She still had her jeans and boots on and he was completely naked. As soon as he finished, he was overwhelmed with shame. He started shaking again, but this time it wasn't good. He was crying.

"What? What? What is it?" Les was crawling back up to him, where he was covering his face with his hands. "Wait? What – what did I do?"

Hal didn't know what to do. He didn't know whether to keep his face covered so she wouldn't see that he was fucking crying, or to put on his clothes and run out of there, or to try to grab onto her and hold her since now she was getting upset. Mostly, he wanted her to shut up because he remembered, sharply, that they weren't alone. He really couldn't deal with maybe Russ and Emma becoming aware that he was buck naked and crying, and now it looked like Les was about to too – her eyes darker, filling with water, and he could see the slightest tremble of her lower lip.

"Shh . . ." he grabbed her hands, and pulled her to him. "Shhh," he held her close, forcing her into the crook of his arm, where she'd be a human heater but he also wouldn't have to look at her.

"What?" She whispered, finally realizing that he was crying.

"I . . . I didn't know you were going to do that."

"Didn't you like it?" she sounded unsure for the first time.

"Yeah, but, I . . ." Hal didn't know how to say what he meant. "I . . ." and he could feel his eyes starting.

"Shhh . . ." Les climbed on top of him, kissing him, and he recoiled a little, could taste himself in her mouth, what she swallowed. He could feel her tense then, and move away from his mouth, burying her face in his neck, her mouth close to his ear. "Tell me, what?"

"You didn't have to do that."

She sat up. Looked him in the eye: "I wanted to."

He broke off eye contact, reached for a loose blanket at the bottom of the bed, pulled it up around them. She returned to lying half on him, half curled around his side, her mouth back by his ear. "I wanted to," but this time it was softer.

"I always thought that that was . . ." he was having trouble finding the words, ". . . demeaning."

"Demeaning?" Les sounded genuinely surprised. She moved her arm beneath the blanket, let her palm rest on his chest, her middle finger making a slow circling motion around his sore nipple.

"Yeah," he sighed, "that to do that, to — was treating a woman like a . . ." He couldn't say it. Les made a sound in the back of her throat, a *hnnh,* like she was hoping he wouldn't finish the sentence. "It just wasn't something a man should do." There, he'd gotten it out. Sort of. She stayed quiet for a minute, more than a minute.

"Hal," and it might have been the first time she'd said his name since they'd met, or the first time he remembered hearing her sat it, "it would have been 'demeaning' if you'd pushed my head down, or made me do something I didn't want to do. But," and now she paused and was maybe trying to find the right words, "I wanted to do it. I liked doing it. I wanted to get you off."

•

After that, they had to keep going out. It was the weirdest hookup he'd ever had. He bet he'd win some sort of competition, but of course he couldn't tell anyone about it. Not even Russ, and they'd been best friends since they were babies. Their moms too. Russ had been there through everything: his mom getting sick and dying, his dad's bullshit, trying the best he could with his brother and sister, and even when he knew he couldn't really do anything and decided that he should go to college, that he needed to that for himself. And Hal knew about Russ and his brother too — about the drugs and rehab, the suicide attempts — but he didn't know what that kind of thing was like when it wasn't just a brother but a twin. Maybe the pain was double then, or maybe Russ felt the pain in his own body, a shadow pain, like his brother was a part of his own flesh and blood. So the story of how he picked up a girl from the rich *Women's College*, got blown, then started crying right after he came would have to be his story and his story alone. Of course, Les teased him about it a little – usually when she began snaking her way down his belly, looking up at him, those dark eyes asking if it was OK now. But she also made sure to note that he owed her an orgasm from that first night, so he'd always owe her.

"Get to work," she'd say, peeling off her jeans. And he would.

•

For spring break, Hal was home for the week, and Les was at loose ends. She was staying at Emma's parents' house, but getting sick of the family togetherness, of sleeping on the pull-out sofa in the den, of putting up with the two cages of parakeets kept in there. Although Emma promised that they'd be quiet once their cages were covered with blankets, they weren't. On the third morning, she woke up coughing, a scratch in her throat, and extracted a stray feather. She called Hal.

He probably should have known better, but he went and picked her up. He thought they'd drive around, get some dinner, and if she wanted, she could spend the night. As they were leaving Emma's, he heard her tell them that she'd be back tomorrow. That was it then.

They drove the east-west roads that broke over the ridges between the lakes; they had to take a scenic route that ringed one of them, but then went back halfway up the lake to cross high on the ridge again. Les had once told him how much she loved these roads. She thought they were beautiful; she said there were no hills where she was from. But all Hal could see were the broken-down houses, the abandoned houses, the yards full of trash, the unlicensed cars with missing doors. People he knew, or people his parents used to know, had lived in these houses once. Some of them were beautiful – old stone and wooden fretwork. But they proved too expensive to keep up, and there were no jobs around. Up on the ridge the wind blew constantly and in winter it was bitterly cold. But when the car crossed the high point of the ridge, the whole lake and valley laid out below and every time they did that, he could hear Les gasp a little; each time, it reminded him of the other times he heard her gasp, the ways he worked to make her make that sound.

He drove her around his town – there wasn't much to see. They sat on the picnic table at the local park, then on the swings. Hal tried to brace her a little for later. She knew his mom died when he was younger, and that his dad was kind of a problem. She knew that he grew up poor. They'd talked about it when Les was feeling left out herself. She'd come from Michigan, and ended up at this small private school upstate, and been surprised by how much money some of her classmates had. She mentioned that in her small town she was considered well-off, but these people were *rich*. Hal had laughed – she didn't know the half of it. City people summered here, and working at the lake resort – bussing tables, cleaning rooms – meant he'd met just about every kind of asshole on the planet.

Les would complain about the rich girls, their cars and their clothes, how they didn't have part-time jobs but always had money. Her first semester she'd taken a horseback riding class, for her phy ed credit, and had to borrow a pony. The Greenwich girls had their own horses stabled on campus. They showed up in those fancy pants that horse girls wore, little hats, and perfect white shirts; she wore jeans and a t-shirt, didn't know how to saddle her horse, or give it the bit. The other girls rolled their eyes at her, how skittish she was to go under the horse's belly and tighten the straps, how she jumped whenever it stamped its feet. Somehow, Les seemed to think she and Hal had something in common when she told these stories. Empathy could only get a person so far.

The minute they walked into his house, Hal knew it was worse than he'd thought. The air was cold inside, and smelled stale.

"Shit," he murmured.

"What?" Les asked, still bundled in her coat in the small hallway, her bag slung over her shoulder.

"Um . . ." Hal stalled for time. Listening, he realized no one else was home, or, no one but his dad. "Can you wait here for a sec?"

"Sure."

He returned from a quick walk down the hallway, looking into his dad's room. "No one's here," He flipped on the lights. The kitchen was still pretty clean, only a few glasses in the sink, some empties in the trash. "Have a seat . . . I just need to check something."

"Oh, Ok." Sitting down at the kitchen table, he could see her relax a little.

"There's probably beer in the fridge," he called over his shoulder as he went down the basement stairs.

In the basement, he checked the fuses, checked the furnace, checked everything else he could think of − there wasn't any heat. Back upstairs Les had opened a beer, but still had her coat on. He shuffled through the pile of mail on the counter: sure enough, months' worth of unopened bills from the local utility. He opened the most recent. Stamped across it was "Final Notice." During the winter months, they couldn't shut off the heat, no matter how behind his dad got with payments. But it was March now, March. When Hal was still living at home, he would have been on top of this, would have called to set up a payment plan, made sure they had heat, made sure that he and his sister and brother were all right. But with him away at college, it had slipped his mind.

"So, . . ." he turned to Les, "the heat's been shut off." He watched her swallow the beer that was in her mouth. She looked at him and didn't say anything.

"I'll get it fixed tomorrow, but . . ." he looked at the stove, figured they could turn that on, thought about how they'd have to cuddle together under an extra weight of blankets, "for tonight we might have to improvise." He could see her thinking. Even though they'd been dating for months, he still couldn't figure out what she was thinking most of the time. Luckily, she usually told him.

"We could make our own heat . . ."

He liked that about her. "We could," he grinned back at her.

"What about your family?"

"My dad's passed out," Her face readjusted, she took another drink from the bottle. "No one else is here." He didn't know where his sister and brother were. He never did anymore – he'd barely seen them since he'd been home. His brother was a senior in high school, always with friends, away from the house as much as he could – Hal couldn't blame him. His sister was younger, only fourteen, but she too wasn't at home much. When he'd seen her lately, she been wearing so much make up he barely recognized her. He didn't know if she had friends, or boyfriends, but she answered in monosyllables or didn't answer at all when he asked her questions. Yesterday, when he asked her where she was going, she'd practically snarled *You're not Mom*! As if he didn't know that.

•

But Les's mood changed later when she saw his bedroom. He could see it on her face the minute they crossed the threshold. His bed was a mattress on the floor, and he'd gathered an armful of extra blankets, that smelled of mothballs and cedar, from the hall chest. But it was the hole. She stopped and looked at it a long time, not saying anything, and then sat on the far end of the mattress, facing away from it. That night, after, she laid next to him like always, but with her back pressed against him. He couldn't see her face. She slept, and dressed, and walked out in the morning, and as far as he could tell, she kept her back to it the whole time. She never asked about it.

He'd kind of forgotten about the hole – it had been there so long, it was just part of the room. When he was little, seven or eight maybe, he'd been angry at something (he couldn't even remember what) and punched that hole in the wall. In the years after, he began worrying it, crumbling the edges of the plaster until it was large enough for him to crawl into. At the edges, the remnants of wooden lathe showed like a large-scale crosshatch drawing. He'd crawl in and hide in the crawl space when his mom and dad got to fighting loudly and he was scared; when he heard voices and volumes asking, demanding, crying, then go quiet. In the crawl space, the hot water pipes ran to the upstairs bathroom, so it was always warm. Once his sister discovered it, she'd use it, too, to hide from the same kind of sounds. Later, when their mom started dying, his little sister would come into his room, her hair all sleep-crazy and ask if they could go into the hole. Sometimes they'd sleep in there all night.

Now, his bed was pressed up against it, and sometimes his pillows kind of blocked it, but he liked the hole being there, had never tried to fix it. It reminded him that he could be angry too, and what anger could do. It reminded him not to grow up to be like his dad. Before she got sick, his dad had been an angry drunk, using his fists on his mom. Hal needed to remember not to be that kind of man. The hole reminded him of what was in him: even when he was little, he could get so angry he could punch a hole in the wall. That that meant he could grow up to be like his dad, throwing fists against anything soft. Les's back turned away from him in the night.

After his mom's diagnosis, his dad's anger turned inward, and the drinking got worse, but then he just started passing out earlier and withdrawing from all of them. The hole reminded him of that too.

He missed his mom. She was so beautiful. He knew the way her eyes looked was mostly from tired and crying and no sleep, but it made her like some kind of goddess. When she started to lose weight, she became honed somehow – bird bones and thinned blue skin. She'd pace around the house, a scarf wrapped tightly around her head, arguing with the utility company to turn the heat back on, and she taught Hal how to use the oven for heat and leave the door open a crack so the kitchen would be warm for meals together. She'd layer on wool socks and sweatpants and a sweater, wrapping her robe around herself, and after Dad passed out, either she or Hal would cover him with an extra blanket and just leave him alone.

•

The next time he saw Les was at Russ's brother's funeral, two months later. His twin had driven his car into the path of an incoming semi one early morning, finally succeeding where other methods had failed him. She and Emma had come together, and sat in the back of the church. As Russ's family was walking up the aisle to take their reserved spots at the front, Russ stopped by Hal, who was sitting by himself. Russ nudged Hal's arm and angled his chin, signaling that he join the family. The music played was very non-churchy – some

Pink Floyd, and the Smiths. After the service, Russ and Hal walked toward the back of the church together, arms around each other, toward the outside where the sun was shining, and the trees were budding. Hal nodded ever so slightly at Les. Tears were streaming down his face and because it was so bright she could see how he looked when he cried.

How to be Gentle

How to paddle a canoe at night: be soundless. Dip your paddles smoothly, so as not to disturb the quiet. When paddling, alternate sides. The person in the stern steers. The person in the bow navigates. Watch the patterns of fog lifting off the water. This could be romantic – the sky starless and suffused a soft blue. Some small talk, not much. An occasional fish breaches the calm of the lake. But it's not romantic. You're in the front, and Mark doesn't know how to steer, switches sides too often.

•

How to get a job: take your newly-minted degree with you, even though you won't need it. Have a carefully-written resume, though you won't need it. You're landlocked for a while, so use word-of-mouth, end up at the home where your grandmother lives. 'Stays' might be a more appropriate word. The plan had been that you would move in and care for her for a time, but she isn't there anymore. You'd already been dreaming of the lake, the low-lying walk-out to the dock, the summer and fall while you took your time planning what's next. But you thought you'd be there together.

•

How to tell a CBRF from a nursing home: A community-based residential facility (per Wisconsin regulations) is a place where residents receive care above the level of room and board, with up to three hours of nursing care per day. Some provide services for people with Alzheimer's and related dementia. This is the kind your grandmother lives in. CBRFs tend to have fewer beds than nursing homes, with smaller resident-to-caretaker ratios, and more of a home-like setting. The people living in them don't usually have needs greater than intermediate nursing care. When you interview for the job, you don't have a CNA license or any relevant experience. When the administrator asks why you want to do this kind of work, you are honest: Your grandmother lives there and you want to care for her.

•

How to live with loneliness: Read books. Drink. Smoke. Make friends with the neighbors who used to be friends with your grandparents. Go to the bar and bring someone home, but never the same person. Binge-watch movies, the blue light of the TV screen filtering over you, over the living room, the carpet and couch and pillows. Pick up extra shifts, take shifts for your co-workers, begin working third shifts. Develop an unorthodox sleep schedule where you can't sleep at all (roaming the lake house, looking out the windows), or can sleep any time, or all the time. Learn to manage the canoe by yourself, sitting in the middle and switching sides. Lean back on the PFD pillows you've wedged against the gunnels and watch the sky. Learn to sleep, morning and midday, on the dock, with a faded life-jacket for a pillow, spreading your hands over your eyes to block the noon sun.

•

How to remove a tick: You can try the tricks using rubbing alcohol or Vaseline or dish soap or essential oils to drown it out or make it unbury itself and back out of the skin, but the way that works best is to grasp as well you can (with fingers or good tweezers) and pull gently. Don't twist. This works with wood ticks, mostly. You'll remember searching for and finding them when you were little. The minor panic that ensued until your grandmother calmed you down and taught you how to remove them. The other kind – the small ones known as deer ticks – are almost impossible to find. After, they leave mark-reddened circles, the tell-tale bulls-eye, and then you watch for a low-grade fever that doesn't go away, or weakness in the limbs. Years and years later, symptoms of memory loss, confusion, agitation or person-ality changes, may appear.

•

How to feed your grandmother: Take whatever was made & puree each ingredient separately, so it's palatable – easy to gum & swallow. Arrange on a plate around the rim, pre-serving some semblance of a meal, preserving her dignity. Ferry small bites to her mouth. Listen to how she hums; watch how she opens her mouth at the spoon's approach. Catch the slight dart of her eyes down to the plate that signifies "more." Take whatever time you need, even if it means an empty dining room, all the other residents having eaten and been re-settled into their rooms. Even if it means your co-workers are well into completing evening cares you have yet to attend to. You've stored up goodwill taking the shifts they don't want.

•

How to manage a morning: Tell whoever's in your bed to leave. Make a pot of strong coffee; nurse two cups. Take a cup over to the neighbor's and sit in the lawn chair, watching your grandmother's friend's cigarettes burn & ash, her own coffee grow cold. Talk some. Watch the no-wake lake and its constellation of fishing boats, an occasional canoe. Watch the small group of men in their pulled-up athletic shorts & knee socks collect and circle for their morning walk. Hear the turn in her voice as small talk makes its way to something else, some buried complaint as she mistakes you for your grandmother, the years wilting away.

•

How to be respectful: When he asks you if you believe in God, switch sides. When he asks if you go to church, tell him you work the Saturday overnight shift. When you notice his face when he sees the beer in your hand, begin being more cautious when you know he'll be visiting. One morning, your neighbor told you he was born again. That he was single but looking for the Virgin Mary. "Good fucking luck," she'd said. You'd noticed Mark only came to the lake on his own, on weekends when his other siblings, the pack of nieces & nephews, weren't there. You'd noticed that just as often he'd be sitting in the side-by-side lawn chair with his mother – the one you usually sat in – but with a discarded coffee cup, a little nest of long-ashed Kents at her side. When your neighbor started telling sad stories, you learned to make a glottal sound in the back of your throat, neither assent or dissent, signaling only that you were listening. You learned to have your hands empty of bottle of beer or glass of wine when Mark stopped over by your deck. Mark was the only one who ever asked after your grandmother. "My mom misses her," he said once.

·

How to bathe your grandmother: Carefully transfer to the shower chair in the walk-in shower stall that has no lip and the sloping tiled floor. Ask for help with the transfer. Slowly remove her clothes – the elastic-waist pants, the sweatshirt with adaptive buttons sewn, the soft ribbed tank tops that fit easily over her head, over her arms that are difficult to move as she holds them bent and close like wings. Check the water temperature carefully on the sensitive inside of your arm. Watch her face for signs of discomfort. Use the handheld shower wand and begin with her feet so as not to startle her. Work slowly. If you wet a washcloth, wring it out, and place it carefully over her forehead and closed eyes, she sometimes smiles.

·

How to keep a secret: When she tells you, you make the throat sound and keep your eyes soft-focused on the lake.

You bum one of her cigarettes. You watch her husband leave, keep listening, watch him come back. You've become attuned to the underbelly of anger in her voice. "Mark knows," she tells you. She tells you how he learned to count and counted the too-short gap between his sister's age and their wedding date. Your grandmother knew. She says the only time your grandmother got mad at her was when she told her to "knock off the Penelope routine." There are two secrets, and you suspected neither. There wasn't much love between your neighbor and her husband, and there was too much between your grandmother and grandfather.

•

How to live with shame: Don't look away. Study the evidence – the bruises, scratches, and skin tears. Think about the tenderness of her body, its weight & balance. Think about how you overestimated your ability and the resulting sound of her hitting metal bars of the home bed and wheelchair. The hunch of her on the floor. The long seconds you stayed still knowing you'd dropped her, misjudging the edge of bed during the transfer. The weeks to months it takes for her skin to heal.

There are different kinds of skin tears, and all are difficult to heal. If the skin flap survives, and is pink and healthy, it can be wrapped and may reclose. This is rare. Elderly skin tears easily, being dry, fragile. Even adhesive bandages can cause skin tears, much less fingernails, or a fall. Once a skin tear happens, the only thing you can really do is keep the wound clean. The only thing you can do about skin tears is prevent them. But even a gentle touch, a little careless, causes them.

•

How to be gentle: When she comes over that morning, she'll put her hand on your shoulder, and take the chair next to you, sit on your deck for a change. You'll have been at the CBRF for two days, your grandmother going, looking like she's gone – no waking, no eating, and it seemed even the kidneys shutting down under cover of fever. You'd held her hand as much as you dared, (some of her bruising still fading), and said things aloud and under your breath, telling her it was okay, that it was time to go. The supervising nurse checked in many times, as had the doctor. Then after two days and a night, her fever broke, and she needed changing, restless in her bed and she was back to the self she'd been, what self was left. You'd left then and gone out and brought home someone, but someone you'd brought home before. Before he left he'd had a cup of coffee, found the sugar in the cupboard. You'd watched him finish before telling him to leave. On the deck, your neighbor put her hand on your shoulder and said, "I've seen that car before." You make the sound in your throat, and sip from your mug. She laughs, "Gives us something else to talk about."

Dogged Problems

When each of his girls were born, after they were cleaned up and swaddled in a newborn blanket, and placed in his arms, he experienced a moment of panic. He wouldn't say he wanted boys, or was only hoping for sons, but raising girls terrified him. He didn't know if he could be a good father to them, what kind of a father he'd be. But he hoped it would be okay, that they'd figure it out together. Ella arrived first, all self-sufficiency, walking and talking early, her first word "No," her first sentence "Me do." Lisa was different right away, in a thousand small ways. She learned "mine" and tried to carve out a life separate from her older sister.

When people asked about the girls now, he brought out his phone and clicked right to Ella's website, was proud to tell people she was a "designer" – thumbed through her portfolio of projects and book covers. He bought every book she worked on, so had an impressive library of experimental poetry and fiction from Midwestern writers, Pushcart winners, and emerging voices she said would be important in coming years. He tried to read as much as he could, but had to admit that much of it was over his head. His favorite covers he arranged facing out so he could look at the interaction of text and color that his baby had made.

And Lisa was a great mom. After college, she returned home and married the boy she'd dated senior year of high school. They had three children: two boys and a girl. They lived in the same town and went to the same church as he and his wife. They babysat often, had get-togethers with the in-laws, were one big extended family. When they planned an event for one of the kids' birthdays, or a holiday like 4th of July, he'd always mention inviting Ella. Usually his wife answered that it was a "family" event, and that Ella didn't have a family. No husband, no kids.

He texted Ella often, and they kept in touch despite distance. He'd take a weekend and go up to see a Twins game, stay in her apartment. Once he even went out with her and her friends, met the "girls" and made a *Sex & the City* joke. They all cracked up – asked him how he knew about that show. Sometimes, late at night when he couldn't sleep, he'd watch the reruns and try to figure out if that's what his older daughter's life was like. Some of it made him blush, but he did hope that she had friends like on the show, and that she had fun like that, although he hoped her love life was less fraught. If she was going to find someone, he hoped it was someone like that Aiden character. Not Big. But he never said any of this to Ella.

•

The island of apples was once home to nine sisters, in some of the earliest versions of the tales. But the most well-known was Morgan, or Morgana, Morgan le Fay. She was a sister – to Morgause, half- or step- to the Arthur of legend, maybe part of some sacred lineage. She served as lady-in-waiting, erstwhile sister to the Queen. Depending on the telling, she was a healer or a sorceress; a smart and gifted girl, good with math, or a seductress engendering intrigue, sowing discord between her brother's knights. She may have killed her brother-King – she may have saved him, taking his body back to Avalon for some future resurrection. If you find yourself in Fairyland, try to keep track of the hours, the days. Once you've passed via some portal into this other place, you'll lose yourself, and if ever you return home, so much time will have passed.

•

Ella loved her work, always had. She was excited about each new project, so even when she wasn't at work, she tended to be thinking about it. She worked for a small firm, taking on all sorts of projects: logo design, graphics, animation, and even some more artistic work – doing hand-drawn art and then scanning it in, using programs to manipulate her designs but create something unique. Although her parents had worried when she majored in art, she'd gone back for a Masters' program that combined computer design and business skills and been hired right away. Her project manager noticed her work ethic, complimented her creativity, and didn't mind if she freelanced on the side. In the last few years, several of the small presses in the cities had contracted her to design their book covers.

She'd been living in St. Paul for twelve years, going home only for Christmas, sometimes Thanksgiving, and maybe a summer visit. The summer between her little sister Lisa's sophomore and junior year of college she'd taken an extended vacation for a month, and worked remotely, after her mother called and asked, and then (likely unbeknownst to her mother) her father had too. No one seemed to know what was going on with Lisa, but the report was that the engagement was off, she rarely left her room, and now she was talking about changing her major. Ella had mostly ignored the call from her mother – her mother seemed to always be concerned about Lisa, and for some reason, think that Ella was interested in the minutia of her sister's life. But a call from her dad was serious.

"Ella," her dad's voice was quiet as usual.

"Hi Dad," Ella looked across her cluttered desk, to where her co-workers were beginning to gather up their things: bags, the cardigans they kept for the summer air conditioning, tablets or laptops. The summer-sun-length-ened day beckoned out the windows; she was planning on meeting some friends for drinks. Tom, her project manager, caught her eye and smiled.

"Ella, I'm calling about Lisa," her father sighed on the phone, and another silence ensued.

"Oh –" Ella answered her father's silence with her own.

"I know your mother called you already, but, I just . . ." he paused, "I just wanted to also ask if you'd consider coming home."

Ella took a moment and swallowed. Her father waited.

"Let me talk to Tom," and at his name mentioned, Tom perked up and smiled again, "and I'll see what I can do."

"Thanks Honey," her father's voice dropped, relaxed. "I just don't know what else to do."

•

Growing up, Lisa had been the pretty one and Ella had been the smart one: simple as that. That's how their mother had referred to them since they were little, five years apart. In school, Ella had done everything first, so when Lisa met her teachers the expectations were set high. Lisa resented this, and Ella had resented her mother's doting on her little sister's cuteness, her popularity, her cheerleading and boyfriends. Ella had been happy to get away for college, and farther away for graduate school, and then find a job the requisite four hours from home. Ella thought four hours was a healthy buffer zone. Whenever she met a woman like Lisa, a woman who was naturally beautiful and used that instead of her brains, who leaned on her looks, Ella would pity her a little and nurse her childhood grudge. But then whatever had happened to Lisa had happened to Lisa. Ella still wasn't sure what that was – despite spending three weeks at home, trying to get her sister to leave her room, do things with her, even asking her out for drinks or the movies, Lisa kept up her guard. Finally, Ella shrugged her shoulders, hugged her mom and dad and went back to her own life.

Now, in her late thirties, the women like Lisa were disappearing and Ella was starting to think that maybe it hadn't been so easy to be the beautiful one after all. She'd worked with a few Lisa's over the years. Most of them had gotten married, had a few kids, and even if they'd come back to work after maternity leave, they either telecommuted part of the time, or left for larger firms. Somehow they never

55

seemed to quite become a part of the family that was the culture at their small company. One Lisa ended up having a relationship with the project manager Tom, and that ended up ending spectacularly badly – for the Lisa, that is. She left, and Tom stayed on. And since the Lisa's changed – they got older and their beauty wasn't as perfect anymore – Ella seemed to change too. When she looked in the mirror now, she found herself staring at herself, more confident than she'd been in the past. She had a good job, was talented and in demand, passionate about what she did. Because of her work with authors, she got invited to readings and book launches, so got to meet writers, editors and publishers, and was around her people – smart, interesting people. Around them, she felt smart, interesting – and attractive. She'd get asked out for drinks, enjoy some good conversation, and sometimes something more. Sometimes she imagined this was what she was missing out on when she was younger – when she let the pretty girls have all the fun.

Something else had changed though too – when she and her friends went out for work they wondered if it had always been this way, or if they were just hyperaware of it now. One of her friends catalogued a series of microaggressions from her boss, all the times he infantilized her, or called her nicknames, diminutives. She went to Human Resources, and they were in mediation. Now she reported to another supervisor, a woman. Another friend left her job to escape the toxic work environment where she was the only woman. Another told about how she was interviewing for a new hire, and one of her peers had the audacity to bring up the dangers of hiring a woman, the potential for a future lawsuit, especially as this woman was conventionally attractive. Ella thought about Tom, how he championed her work in a way that seemed over-the-top sometimes, and how it had started to make her uncomfortable. Lately she'd been wondering whether he was really a fan of her work, or whether he was a fan of her. Lately, she'd been thinking about the Lisa, trying to remember the way he'd interacted with her before that had all started, while it was going on, when it had gone bad.

"Basically," her friend Gwen said, "it's exhausting!" She was waving her half-empty drink in one hand, trying to signal the bartender with the other.

They were out, like they were most Thursday nights, at a little bar downtown from Gwen's office, Minnesota Public Radio headquarters. It was usually four of them: Gwen, Tina who worked for the city, Ella, and Shawn who taught in a charter school. They were all functionally single – most of them still, but Shawn had been briefly married in her twenties. Tina had a partner, but she worked second shift.

"It is," Tina piped up. "If I'm not praised for my good work, I worry I'm being ignored because I'm a woman. But if I get too much attention, I suspect ulterior motives."

"Me too," Gwen answered, as the bartender approached.

"Does anyone else feel weird saying 'me too' lately? Like, if you say 'me too' you're saying #metoo?" That was Ella.

Shawn answered, "I've started saying 'I concur' or 'yo tambien' . . ." She laughed. "Now I hear my students saying, 'I concur'!" She lifted her glass when the bartender motioned at the rest of the table.

Ella thought about Tom again – about the special projects he seemed to line up more and more often lately, projects for just the two of them. She thought about how often these seemed to necessitate later nights in the office, ordering take-out, and working past the natural light's extinction beyond the glass walls until they were both soft-lit by desk lamps and monitor screens. There had been a few times when she'd taken a slow breath, feeling him standing close next to her, and once when he'd been leaning over her shoulder to look at her two designs side-by-side on the screen, he'd gently picked up her hair and lifted it from her shoulder and neck, moving it to the side, so he could see better. She'd felt his knuckles graze the skin under her ear. Next month, the two of them were going to a work conference together, traveling and staying in a hotel for three days. He'd made the arrangements; the firm was paying for it.

•

Changelings move between our world and the land of Fairy. There are various stories why this might be – fairy children need human milk. Fairy folk desire human beauty. To catch a changeling, watch it when it doesn't know it's being watched: changelings often exhibit remarkable intelligence and special abilities. When left alone, they will astound with their song and dance. They possess prodigious appetites, never satisfied, never full. Some changelings forget their origins, and live forever as humans. Those who remember though may leave – empty beds and empty rooms as reminders behind them, parents bereft of even that false child.

•

Lisa's first semester of college, one of the big projects was a "dogged problem" – it was in the class that was supposed to teach them about college, about thinking, about approaching questions with deeper and deeper layers of complexity. First, read an article looking for the main issues: what's the primary question and possible answers – summarize that. Then, look at the author: who are they? What is their background? What about their education, interests, identity might affect the way they're looking at the topic? Next, consider the contexts of the article. Each time reading the article, look at a new layer – there are concentric layers to be analyzed, to be understood. It took Lisa all semester, and she still didn't understand really, but by end, she understood what her professor wanted of her, and learned to go through the motions. She made herself a little cheat-sheet to get her through the class.

Finally, she hit on an analogy of sorts: it was like the way she learned to do her makeup, using the little palette of beiges to create highlights and hollows, cheekbones and shadows – what was called contouring. One of her soon-to-be sorority sisters taught her how that same semester, during rush week, when she took Lisa aside one Tuesday night, asked if she could "do" her face. She told her she *could be so pretty*. Lisa had thought she already was.

But Katrin had spent a few hours straightening and smoothing her hair; using layers of liquid foundation, then the little palette to create a new face for her, before even beginning with colors for her eyes & lips & a blush for her cheeks. She'd plucked not just the hairs between her brows, but up and under the arches too, creating a curve that arced over the brow bone (and having to color in that palest of white skin too). With her new face, Lisa hadn't recognized herself at first, but she'd known that what Katrin had done was called "strobing" (she'd seen a YouTube tutorial) and a "daytime smoky eye." She'd spent the next weekend in her dorm room, practicing and practicing to re-create the look; applying, then washing off the makeup, re-applying, learning to watch the danger zone between chin and neck for the telltale tell of missing blend.

She'd met Isaac that semester, at her first frat party. She'd been accepted into the sorority, along with Katrin. By fall break, when she'd visited home for the first time, and had to ask for spending money from her parents, she hadn't yet learned to apply the lessons of the dogged problem outside of the classroom, but she would soon. When her mother saw her face, her new face, her smile fell and it had taken her a moment to re-focus – to recognize that the young woman standing before her was her daughter, her littlest girl, who'd just left for college a few months before, with a series of duffel bags full of jeans and hoodies and t-shirts, all soft and worn. Lisa's mother still wore her tan pants, what she called "chinos," and loose button-down women's shirts, with a little embroidery here and there. Her hair was always in a bob, and sometimes she'd get a little low-lighting done, to counteract the grey that washed her out. She didn't understand how or why her daughter would be needing all new clothes after just a few months, or looking like a completely different person. She'd always thought her Lisa was beautiful just the way she was. She'd spent years telling Lisa that, telling everyone else too.

•

Isaac was on the basketball team, a starter — lean, with muscles that looked like cramped fists in his upper arms. When he held himself above her, Lisa would reach out and squeeze them sometimes if they were being playful. If they were having sex, she didn't do much of that, depending on why they were having sex — if it was after a win, he'd be tired but amped up with celebration, so everything would be very quick. If they lost, she'd be extra quiet, but try to cover him with kisses, moving her mouth down his body and taking his mind off the game. They dated for a year and half, got engaged early spring semester of his senior year; Lisa was a sophomore, holding more or less steady at a B average.

Isaac had taught her about fundamentals, the importance of drills. Lisa had added this to her cheat-sheet about the dogged problem, her weekend of practicing makeup tutorials, had learned the way to wheedle spending money out of her parents — inviting them up to home games to see her boyfriend play, to meet her new friends, to sit with the sorority sisters and their well-dressed fraternity brother boyfriends, to join them all for dinner before the games, and then hug and kiss them goodbye after the game. After the game, the night would become a blur: plastic cups, and basements with sticky floors, Lisa and the sisters ushering the new pledges and their friends around, showing them the ropes. Lisa would keep her eye out for a girl like her, a girl with potential who just needed a nudge, a little extra time – a little training, a little motivation. The way Isaac took some of the younger teammates under his wing, introducing them to the math and reading tutors, playing interference with coach, hustling them out of the parties if the cops showed, or things got out of hand.

Things started to get out of hand for Lisa the first semester of her sophomore year, when she finally took the classes she'd been putting off, required for the core, but rumored to tank GPA's. First, she'd read the assignment sheets for the papers. Then, she'd do her study of the professors: Who are they? What are their interests? What about their identities might affect the way they approach the class, grading? Lisa could be dogged too, when she knew what she wanted. Soon she'd convince her mother it was a good idea to accept a ring from Isaac, before he graduated, to consider it a down-payment for the rest of their lives. *Besides*, she'd say, when she and her mother were talking, in the dim candlelight over a stained tablecloth of a restaurant back home, *didn't you and Dad meet in college?*

With the bioethics professor, she'd always submit a draft of her papers early – something he suggested in the syllabus. And he'd always meet with her to discuss where she was unclear, where her argument was weak, where her citations were incorrectly formatted. Some things she could fix, but some things he said she just couldn't understand. She'd sit at the round table in the library, in the quiet study room, and move her eyes back and forth from where he scribbled his notes in the margin, and try to follow his explanations of what he meant. She knew to nod, and to smile, and to turn everything in on time – or early. She knew if she kept doing everything she could that he wouldn't grade her too harshly. She'd wear him down.

But she wasn't dogged enough. Her mid-terms came back with two B-minuses – one in bioethics, one in World literature.

•

Three years later, she'd walk, cap and gown – hair immaculately straight, face perfectly contoured. Her mother sat beside her father in one of the metal folding chairs, under the stretched white fabric of the tent, where the entire crowd had sunk a few inches into the ground as they'd settled in. Grass a vibrant spring green, but the lawn softened from days of rain, a mini monsoon. In the lowest spots, particle board was laid down and chairs and feet stayed dry; luckily it had been cool enough that no mosquitoes hatched yet. Lisa's left ring-finger was bare, walking the poured sidewalk that served as the processional aisle. She'd given the ring back not long after she'd got it, not long after Isaac graduated, not long after the end-of-the-year party at Isaac's frat.

•

Lisa had had her eyes closed, running her hands over muscles like clenched fists in his arms and when she opened her eyes it wasn't Isaac. Or she thinks that's what happened.

Maybe she hadn't known it wasn't Isaac until later, until the next morning, until she'd woken and pulled on a t-shirt from the floor and run into Katrin in the hallway and her friend had been laughing, a little bleary-eyed, but looked at Lisa like she'd looked at her that first semester: like she couldn't believe she was so stupid.

She must have been drunk. He must have taken advantage of her, the captain of the basketball team who always pushed Isaac around, the accidental fouls that were a little too often to be accidents. She'd talked to Katrin, Katrin had talked to her RA, the RA had come to her room with a brochure and a list of questions. Isaac wasn't answering her texts or snaps. She'd told them what she remembered, which wasn't much. But they'd moved fast, interviewing other people from the party and it all fell apart quickly. Everyone talked about how drunk she was, how drunk everyone was, no one knew what really happened. They told her, after an initial "investigation" there wasn't enough to proceed, but gave her information about counseling. She went home. She waited for her grades, and the letter that confirmed she was on academic probation. She waited to hear from Isaac. When she didn't, she mailed him his ring back.

•

Stories of knights, dragons, fairies, anything set in a liminal place, can be made to work allegorically. Spenser's *The Faerie Queene* is about Queen Elizabeth, but also the Church of England. Lisa's mother met her father during a literature class, and she nicknamed him Redcrosse – he always seemed to bumble around, needing her help to get out of this or that fix, find his way again. He was the same way when the girls were born. When Lisa told them about the ring, they worried. They weren't sure about this Isaac, and definitely thought they were both too young to be engaged. But Lisa was persistent. And her mom was proud of her daughter's tenacity – for the first time, maybe, she seemed a little like Ella.

•

After the graduation ceremony, the professors lined up in a kind of gauntlet, clapping and congratulating the students as they filed past, their tassels flipped to the other side. Beneath her thin acrylic gown, Lisa was carrying twenty extra pounds, the weight she'd gained after sophomore year. She'd become the kind of girl people described as having a "pretty face," the kind of girl who wore cold-shoulder tops that were loose around the belly, tunic style, with leggings. As she passed her bioethics professor in the gauntlet, he smiled and mouthed *Congratulations*. She set her eyes on the end of the line of faculty in their robes and stoles, the sidewalk continuing to a smaller tent, staffed by work-study students holding napkins, orange coolers with bottled drinks, and platters of cookies, where she could just make out her parents, waiting.

•

Ella was working at the central work table with two of her colleagues and the new intern from the arts college, going over the final proposal for a client. Her cell rang and displayed her father's number. She answered and walked toward the wall of glass, looking out over the shadowed street.

"Hi, Honey," her father's voice sounded tired.

"Dad, what's up?"

"I'm in the hospital, waiting on some test results – your mom will probably call you later."

"Is Mom there?"

"She's getting coffee or something . . . probably calling Lisa right now." Ella winced a little. She'd grown used to her mother's preference for her little sister, but it still hurt. She knew her dad tried to make up for it, in ways large and small, like right now, calling her, ensuring she wasn't left out of the loop of whatever was going on.

"What kind of test results?"

"Well, they won't be in for a few days yet, but I already know . . ." his voice sounded resigned.

"What Dad?" Ella was leaning up against the long panes of glass, bracing herself for whatever came next. The middle-of-the-day phone call. The subterfuge. The way his voice sounded. The subtle dig at Mom.

"I'm pretty sure it's cancer. It won't be good. I haven't been feeling good for a long time, not since Easter really, but I didn't want to tell your mother – she's been so busy with the grandkids – and at first it was just some belly pain, and . . ." he continued, telling her about what felt like indigestion, and then became sharper, and how he started losing weight and how much he'd lost. Ella was putting all her weight on the glass panels now, eyes closed, the phone pressed to her ear. The sounds of the office behind her had disappeared, muted, and her office mates returned to their tasks – only the intern seemed keyed on his supervisor's distress: the way her shoulders were hunched, her head tucked so the cords of her neck showed tensed up above the neckline of her shirt. Ella was still listening to her father, but thinking about how she hadn't gone home that summer for a visit, hadn't been home since Christmas, so hadn't seen him to notice anything. He hadn't come for a visit either, and she hadn't thought much of it, being busy lately with her new supervisory duties, and other things.

"Honey?"

"I'm here, Dad."

"Keep talking to me for a while until your mom comes back, OK? Or the doctors."

"Sure Dad."

"But let's talk about something else, OK?"

"Sure."

"I'm reading *The Land of the Faes*." Ella perked up, raising her head again, and looking out the windows across the bit of the downtown she could see. She even laughed a little.

"You are?"

"Yeah, but I don't get it . . . beautiful cover, though. I did like the part about the eels."

Ella did the cover for Cinderstack Press, one of the Twin Cities up-and-coming small presses. She'd been glad to get a project from them – was hoping to do more. Their authors had won a couple National Book Awards in the last few years, and been shortlisted for a Pulitzer. This last year they'd even opened a brick and mortar store – reversing a trend. That was where they'd held the book release party, a converted warehouse with overhead garage doors that could be opened to the sidewalk for events, where Ella had met the author: Devin.

Lately, the cover trend for books had foregrounded the title: a serif font in a bold color (often white) on a contrasting background. Sometimes the letters would reveal a pattern behind them. Those books look great on bookshelves, but aren't much for designers or authors to dream of. Ella wanted to do something else with *The Land of the Faes* – although she could imagine how she could manipulate the letters, casting the capital "L," the "F" in relief against some carefully-chosen tapestry, its perfect form in the perfect font. The book demanded something different: it was a story unlike anything else she'd ever read. It started one way, with one kind of story – a character who seemed like she might be the protagonist – but ended up being a completely different kind of story, with completely different kinds of characters. The narrative didn't follow any kind of chronology or linear structure, and then there were these strange interludes, like the eels.

In the story, electric eels had power strips along their backs, but they also had additional holes (depending on what bodies of water they lived in) to be useful for voltages and appliances of the nearest peoples and continents. They adapted to new technology with USB ports, and headphone jacks, and iPad chargers, and eventually evolved to become all-in-one charging stations for any and all electronics. The people couldn't adapt – they couldn't overcome their fear of the eels and learn how to harness this electricity. When

Ella's father mentioned that he didn't "get" the book, he meant he couldn't follow the story, follow the characters. When he said he liked the "part about the eels," he meant this parable, the idea that evolution continued in tandem with human needs, but the humans were unable to understand or make use of it.

Ella's father had been right. The tests confirmed advanced pancreatic cancer and gave him forty-five days to two months to live. Ella went home as soon as she could, putting what projects she could on hold, delegating what tasks she could to her capable team, giving her intern (who was very talented, but just needed guidance) more experience than he'd ever hoped for when he applied. In the couple weeks before her dad went into hospice, they'd sit in his study and he'd ask her to explain some of the covers, and some of the books. He learned the difference between fonts, what a serif was. She explained prose poetry. Near the end, once he'd moved to the hospital and was in and out, she'd just read to him — but from his books, the kind of books he'd read to her when she was little: Hardy Boys, and Philip K. Dick, and once when she wasn't sure if he was listening she'd pretended to start *50 Shades of Grey*, and he's started to laugh, quietly, but then started coughing, and hadn't been able to stop and they'd had to call the nurse, so she didn't try that again.

Her mom said she couldn't handle seeing him like that, not at the end, so once Dad moved to the hospice he didn't have any visitors but his oldest daughter. Lisa said she couldn't come because she had to take care of the kids, take care of Mom. When he went, he went quickly, and Ella was there. She climbed into bed and held her father and he died. The last time he'd seen his whole family together was about two weeks before he died: he'd slept all morning, and just taken his pain pills, and Ella had set him up in the recliner with a blanket, and Lisa and her family had come over. The kids seemed afraid of their grandpa, but each had hugged him gingerly, and her mother had paced nervously, offering coffee or cookies. Ella had noticed how quickly her father tired, how much he was trying to keep up appearances for Lisa and her family. For Mom. The blanket Ella had wrapped around him slowly slipped from his lap, falling to the floor; Ella looked at her father's feet, slightly blued from poor circulation, his nails unkempt. He looked so vulnerable, so small. When she crawled into bed and held him at the end, she realized how much weight he'd lost.

•

The first time Ella read *The Land of the Faes* she didn't like it. Thinking about a potential cover design, she didn't even understand what the book had to do with title. She did some research on Fairyland. A place where a woman, or sort-of woman, ruled; people who wandered there lost sense of time – the sky was greyed haze, and no sun visible. Creatures living there were either romanticized or demonized, born of the devil or fallen from grace. The human world and Fairyland touched hands across some barrier between worlds: a hollow or cave, some dip where mist & fog gathered, a reedy place at the edge of a lake – veils between worlds gathered there, heavy-weighted curtains

70

to be opened or closed if someone knew how. Mostly Ella found herself looking at drawings – all the ways these kin had been imagined through the years, all the ways people hypothesized their origins and desires and actions, seeking mirrors. Making mirrors, like some half-understood sibling. Ella read the book again.

When she pitched cover designs to Cinderstack, she argued for artwork that had nothing to do with the pages inside the book. The book cover would be a version of Fairyland, peopled with half-seen creatures hiding behind mossy stumps, small eyes popping up from hillocks, parting tall grass. The reader would be left to wonder if the book was fairy, hovering beyond a veil, only discernible at times, other times unknowable, unnamable. She did a mock-up of the capital letters, drawn like the initials in illuminated man-uscripts, surrounded by pixie rings of mushrooms. Finely-drawn gills showed from underneath the caps – lore had it that if a mortal entered these naturally-forming rings, she could dance with fairies or be transported to the land of Fae. To her surprise, the press loved it. They said the author did too. She hand-drew the font for the title, built out of fey creatures peeking from trees & hollows, appearing out of a smoked-grey background.

At the release party, Ella met the author. Devin looked like a changeling: wide-open green eyes, slight-framed, too beautiful for this world. Curls upon curls. A septum pierc-ing that glittered just beneath their nose. At the podium, they read the chapter about the eels. During the reception afterward, Ella waited until the fans were finished, flagging them down with their newly-bought books asking to be signed. Ella waited until Devin endured the polite small talk with the bookstore people, the press people, and watched a few genuine smiles cross their face when a friend came up for a hug or a kiss. Ella could tell these were friends, true friends, because for those few rare moments in the evening, Devin's face lit up, their copper curls shook, head bobbing along with whatever animated conversation. Still, Ella waited, and when it was just a few people left, and the staff were beginning to draw down the garage-style doors, she went over and introduced herself. Devin's mouth opened in a wide O, and turned the book toward her. They flipped to the acknowledgements at the back and pointed: "To Ella, whom I've never met, but who drew me all over the cover."

When Ella returned home after her father's funeral, she went straight to Devin's apartment, to what would be their apartment soon, and Devin held her while she cried. Leaving the funeral, her mother had said, "I'm glad you won't be alone."

Coursing

Kerri was running late to dinner, but only had two ciga-rettes and knew she'd need more. Her brother's house was another fifteen miles into the dark. She pulled in to the corner gas station at the edge of the small town she grew up in. It used to be a Citgo, then maybe a BP, now it was a no-name station, but had a hand-lettered sign for regis-tering deer. Only one pump appeared to be functioning. A sad car was parked there, sputtering, mismatched side panels and visible Bondo. She went inside. There was a small counter and two dimly-lit aisles that angled toward the back. When the small brass bell made its noise, the man behind the counter stood up.

"Pack of Marb Silvers short," she said. He smiled, meth teeth.

"Credit or debit?"

"Credit," she swiped her card. He took her in: her coat, bag, her sleeked hair and lipstick.

"Can I see your card?" He smiled again. She handed it over.

"Are you related to the Pawlosky's around here?"

"My family," she said. He said her last name differently than she did, the way her family still did: extra weight on the second syllable, spreading each vowel. He was still looking at her. "I was born here," she continued, to appease him.

"You know Terney?" he asked, dubious.

"My brother."

"You're Terney's little sister?" he sounded incredulous. He took a half-step back, looked her up and down, slow. Maybe he was looking for a resemblance, ways she could be her brother's sister, ways she could be part of her family. She held her face neutral, stilled her limbs.

"I don't need the receipt," she put her hand out for her card, signed the store receipt he nudged toward her. "Have a nice Thanksgiving . . ." she said as she turned, and he snorted a laugh. The bell told her departure. At the gas pump outside, the junk car was still running its rough rhythm, its driver alongside, dressed in blood-stained flannel and jeans. The wind blew her carefully-straightened hair, cut and colored and styled once a month.

At her brother's, they had tacos, ground beef and chicken, a choice of flour tortillas or hard shells. Her sister-in-law made flan for dessert. Her nephews and nieces played with the dog and cat, ran down the long hallway, alternated between board games and video games. After dinner, they all ended up back in town at the bowling alley for drinks. The holiday didn't officially begin until tomorrow, so that night they ran into locals and people back visiting family. Kerri saw people she knew from high school, people she was supposed to know from childhood – someone who had taught her swimming lessons as a girl, someone who babysat her, someone whose siblings she'd been in school with.

Some faces she couldn't place, but pretended she did. Her relations re-introduced her around, pointing her out, widening their conversations when she passed by, including her. And if there was blood beneath any fingernails, it was only from the work done in the shed in the lengthening afternoon light; in the cold the meat would keep, and the next day or the next, they'd drop the kill off at the processors.

In the bathroom, she'd carefully check her face: no eye makeup, but allover foundation coverage, a statement lip. She'd reapply liner, matte lipstick, make sure there was no feathering. With some people, Kerri did the conversational dance of figuring out who they knew in common – cousins & classmates & former spouses, until they hit on some tangential connection, enough to sustain a half a beer, or a cigarette out in the cold night air, next to the flower pot filled with butts and trash. Once, not in her hometown, she'd been in the bathroom looking at herself in the mirror over the sinks and caught a woman smiling at her. "Pawlosky, right?" the woman asked. Kerri felt seen, caught out.

"Do I know you from . . .?" and she inserted the name of her small town.

"We were in school together," the woman said. That's all she said, turning around quickly, her smile closed and hard to read, the door swinging behind her.

She didn't live far away, but sometimes it seemed like another world. When she was back visiting, things were eerily familiar, as if she'd never left. But things were also completely different, as if she was fundamentally unhomed. The grocery store had a peculiar smell, as if it hadn't been sufficiently disinfected – she noticed this when her stepmother sent her out for more butter. The side streets were uncurbed, so the barrier between yard and street was ungoverned, colonized by non-running cars and children's toys of yellowing plastic. She slept on a pull-out couch, and woke early to wan morning light, unsure where she was, her niece poking her forehead with her plump finger, asking for the WiFi password.

•

That afternoon, riding in the back of her parents' car to the extended family Thanksgiving dinner, she watched out the side window as the rows of carefully-planted woodlots flickered past. The hunt had begun last weekend, and they'd passed pickups with deer loaded in their beds, mouths open and tongues painfully extended. Partially field-dressed. For hunters who hadn't had luck, the holiday provided mandatory time-off to try again. Here and there, Kerri saw cars and trucks pulled into side roads, the edges of fields, bottomed out in ditches, or just beyond the shoulder; from there, they would have walked in to tree stands and blinds. It was a mild fall, just a hint of frost in the morning. When they were leaving the bowling alley the night before, the first accumulating snow had begun to fall.

By morning, it had mostly burned off the roads, but in the woods there'd still be a slight coating of white on the ground, lacing leaves. Good for tracking. As the woods with their straight leafless trunks passed by, her head leaning against the car window, she saw a hunter walking. Maybe he was on a trail. Maybe he was flushing quarry – there may have been others, working in concert with him, walking a

76

narrowing triangle, moving animals to a point where they could be more easily taken and tagged. Maybe he was onto something he'd already hit, following a spatter of blood on the crystalline white, watching where and how the crimson feathered out – guessing how long it had been since the warm wet fell. Guessing how long since the prey, wounded and in pain, had passed this way. For a brief second, Kerri saw his concentration: his sharp shoulders, the forward-jutted chin, the gun in his hand – his steady feet.

She kept watching out the window. It seemed like only a few frames further. Maybe five-hundred feet. She saw a woman, running. An open rust-colored coat. One shoe. One bare foot. Behind her, a flutter of fabric, torn and trailing. The woman staggered and tripped, hands reaching out, touching tree trunk after tree trunk as she scrambled.

Kerri blinked, came to. She sat up straight, "Dad?"

"We're almost to town," her father answered. He was driving, and dusk was setting in, the headlights stretching long onto the two-lane country road in front of them.

"Dad, I . . ." Kerri looked out the side window again, but couldn't see the woman. She swung around in her seat.

"What is it Honey?" Her father's voice tinged with concern, and her stepmother turned from the front seat to look at her. Kerri looked at her, her father's second wife. These last few years, Kerri had begun to warm to her. Through her father's cancer scares, Kerri's separation from her fiancée, her brother's legal troubles, her stepmother had been a constant: calling and checking in, keeping them all connected, signing off every group email and text with "Love" even when unnecessary. It had gotten to the point where Kerri had begun to believe it.

"I – nothing . . . Nothing."

"You OK?" Her stepmother asked. There were no cars behind them, no headlights to bounce their light up into her eyes, but Kerri thought she saw a little caught glare, a little wetness. At her aunt and uncle's house, the windows would be steamed from all the food coming in and out of the oven and refrigerator, all the mouths opening and closing, the door letting in brothers and sisters and parents and cousins – cousins Kerri hadn't seen since they were kids. There'd be second cousins and third cousins, and cousins removed several times, by distance & divorce. On the table, the turkey skin would glisten, the watered top of the green bean casserole, and three different kinds of cranberry sauce, one bearing the imprint of the can it came in, no matter how her aunt tried to disguise its origin. "Kerri . . .?" Her stepmother was still looking at her.

"Yeah, I just . . ." she looked out the side window again, "Can we stop at the gas station?"

•

At the counter, the same clerk was there, but didn't seem to recognize her. He smiled at her with his darkened disappearing teeth, but didn't ask to see her card. After getting her cigarettes, she turned around, and saw her, the woman in the rust coat. On her feet were two laced up work boots, and above the boots wool socks, and above the socks a shock of pale winter skin before delicate floral fabric and lace. Kerri stumbled forward and the woman reached out to steady her, holding her up with her calloused, sturdy hands. Where her left hand caught Kerri's left hand they shared a birth mark, a small darkened circle on the fleshy part of the palm.

Muscle leans into memory. The curve on County GG where she'd lost control in high school – the curve insufficiently graded, no shoulder, the pine boughs' branching shade that always left an iced patch. Ever since the first skid, she knew to brake before it, even though no yellow sign urged caution. The woman's nails were torn jagged, pressure pinked the half-moons, and the nail beds were stained a dark and dirty brown that could be dried blood. Kerri caught and held the woman's stare, her glittering animal eyes.

The Luck and Misfortune of Others

The minute she turned onto the highway she knew she'd made a mistake. The clouds had been building for the last twenty minutes of the drive, blue layered on blue, but when she listened to the radio reports all the weather advisories were for counties to the south. Indigo clouds stretched over each other, smudged at the edges, and she watched the trees to see whether they shook in any breeze, knowing the temperatures and humidity were ripe for big summer storms. Drops started to blister down as she was on the lake road, ringing between the cottages, but the tall pines caught most of it, sheltering the narrow asphalt and her car, the headlights on at mid-day, but still it seemed just a shower: heavier than she thought, still not much of a storm.

But once she turned onto the highway she couldn't see anything – the windshield wipers full blast, the headlights muffled through the onslaught of water streaming down in waves. The cars driving from town across the causeway between the lakes were pulling off anywhere they could. If she'd pulled off there, into the Doe Run restaurant, its sand volleyball courts drenched with standing water, the flimsy nets buffeted by wind, she could have made a run from the parking lot to the back kitchen door. The locals knew it was never locked, and even though the power had already gone out, there were a few of them in the bar, where they helped themselves to the rail bottles, drinking cheap liquor neat, watching the storm out the high, narrow windows: the wind caught the too-tall, slightly bent red pines, stretching them back and forth like car dealership inflatables, wacky men, waving their improbable arms until they either righted themselves or snapped.

But the turn-off to her mother's house was only another hundred yards down the highway. She'd come for the day, hoping to float at the swimming hole, enjoy a little sun and quiet. Even though she only lived an hour away, she rarely visited – so she took a personal day, packed a paperback novel and a dollar-store inflatable raft and didn't tell anyone she'd be in town. The storm's sudden onslaught reminded her of the tornado when she was little, on this very lake. They'd all huddled in one of the cabin's small bedrooms, the kids under one of the metal-framed beds and she remembered looking up at the mesh wire that supported the mattress, its pungent mildew smell. They'd been down on the lake when someone spotted the water-spout and all run; her aunt was still holding a hot dog as they hunkered in the bedroom, waiting out the funnel that jumped from the lakeshore, dumping its load of water, and landed just beyond the cabin, twisting the tall pines into a furled pattern layered on their cars. She was thinking of that long-ago storm as she tried to drive the last few yards, watching for the road sign, finally turning a hard right into the subdivision.

•

She'd loved that cabin, her grandparents', but it was gone now. Prices of lake frontage rose and rose, and the taxes alone kept most off the lake at all. The cabins were slowly torn down and replaced with houses too big for the lots; the trick was to keep a corner of the original foundation so that the re-built house wasn't considered new construction. What used to be her grandparent's cabin was now some-one's summer house, a second home, only occupied for a few months a year. The wet-smelling mattresses were gone, and the hamper that always held extra swimsuits for any-one who needed one – swimsuits left over from long before her time. Women's suits with skirts and stiffened lining and hard points that made breasts of their own even when no one was wearing them.

Her mother lived in a sub-division across from the lake. Not lake frontage, not lake access, barely lake adjacent. But on a nice night, Mom could walk down to the public land-ing to see the water. Recently she'd gotten a little hand-truck to haul the kayak to the landing. She lived on the other lake, the dammed millpond, but if the water was high enough, a person could paddle under the access bridge into the lake proper and glide past what used to be their frontage.

Once she turned away from the direction of the wind, she could see again, so she kept to the right, following the curve that would get her to her mother's house to wait out the storm. She should check on her anyway: whether she had power, if there were any limbs or lines down. But just as she was nearing her mother's driveway, one of the spruces

– ornamental, fat and squat – in a neighbor's yard, fell right across the road, pulling down the sparking lines. She put the car into reverse and pulled into the nearest driveway, ran from the car into the open garage and knocked on the door.

When it opened, she almost said, "Sanctuary."

•

She'd had to knock twice. The garage was a two-car but only held one, its edges piled with boxes, a mower, snow blower, rakes, shovels and other tools. No one answered the first knock so she knocked again harder, sure by the wide open garage door, that someone was home.

"Hi," she said to the woman, "I was trying to get to my mother's – she lives just a few houses down . . ." The woman didn't smile to ease her explanation. She stood there in the barely opened door, looking her up and down. Her swim suit and skin showing through her cover up. She paused to push the wet hair out of her face. "Can I wait out the storm here?"

The woman looked her full in the face but didn't answer. Her face was tensed, watching the storm out the open garage door, the driving rain and wind, the thunder's sounds concentric and close.

"You can't come in," she finally answered.

Jeannie had already been moving forward, her foot on the first of the steps. She paused, taken aback.

"I don't mean to intrude, but . . ." she faltered. The woman's face was impassive now, some approximation of crossed arms, if crossed arms could translate to a facial expression. "The storm's pretty bad . . . a tree just fell in front of my car on the road. I can't get through." She knew she sounded like she was begging.

"You can wait in the garage," the woman said. From behind her, Jeannie heard another voice, a man's.

"What tree? Where?"

Jeannie tried to talk past the woman, thinking maybe the man would be more sympathetic. She half-shouted over the woman's shoulder, "On the road right past your house! It almost hit me!" The woman flashed angry eyes at Jeannie and shut the door.

Jeannie retreated from the half-step she'd taken towards the house, exhaled. Since when didn't people help in a possible tornado? After the last one, when she was a kid, all the neighbors had gone around checking on each other, making sure people had candles and matches and were all right. Her father and uncles fired up the chainsaws and cut trees and branches into manageable lengths while the teenagers hauled the wood into piles near the ends of driveways. The mothers and aunts took food around and watched each other's kids. After the power company had come through and taken care of the live wires, they'd all piled into the car and driven around town, rubbernecking at the damage until the sun finally went down, alternately awed and hushed by the luck and misfortune of others.

Jeannie should have pulled in at the old cottage, before she even got to highway, knocked on that door and told them she'd grown up there, that this used to be her family's cottage. Those people would have invited her in – let her sit on their big sectional and watch the storm travel across the lake, the curtains of rain transecting the surface of the water into some kind of topographical map. Instead, she hovered just inside the rim of the garage door watching the storm wreak its havoc on the house's backyard. She could smell motor oil, sawdust, gasoline.

She heard the door open behind her and turned. The woman came out and quickly closed the door behind her. Jeannie turned her back and looked out again, where her car was parked behind another car. The rain splattered in, sideways, wetting her feet and legs.

"You don't have to stand there," the woman said. "You can come back here where it's dry." She was wearing dark dress pants of some cheap material, a white shirt, and dress shoes. Work clothes – when she'd first opened the door, Jeannie thought she'd had on some sort of name badge, but it was gone now. She reached toward Jeannie, holding a water bottle. "For you . . ."

Jeannie waved it away, "Do you think I could use the bathroom?"

The woman's face immediately tensed, closed down. "That's not a good idea." She looked past Jeannie again to the open space left by the open garage door. "We lost power just before you showed up."

"Oh," Jeannie didn't know what that had to do with using the bathroom.

"We've been listening to the radio in there," the woman continued, "it's almost over."

"Oh," Jeannie said again, stupidly.

"Do you have your cell phone?"

Jeannie motioned toward her car, parked near the end of the drive, "It's in my car . . ."

"You should always keep that with you," the woman said. "As soon as it lets up, you should get going."

And she did. After a few more minutes, the sky lightened – moving from the deepened blue to a grey-blue to the yellow-green of a washed out sky. Jeannie got back into her car, readying to drive away. The woman had never come back out of the house; it's not like Jeannie wanted to thank her or anything – thank her for what? As she was sitting in the driver's side, looking down the curve to her mother's where the tree marked the blocked path to safety, she saw the man standing on his little cement stoop of a porch, covered by a small triangle of roof. She waved, and he locked eyes for a moment, ducked his head and turned away. Because that could have happened.

•

"Hi," she said to the blonde woman who opened the door, "I was trying to get to my mother's – she lives just a few houses down . . ." she paused to push her hair out of her face. "A tree fell across the road," she motioned in the general direction of the tree. "Can I wait out the storm here?"

The woman smiled and opened the door wider, where a man stood just behind her, turned and looked at him. "Sure," the woman answered, after waiting a beat. "Come in."

"Thank you," she stepped up the cement steps from the garage and into a kitchen. Candles flickered on the countertops, and the wan storm light filtered through a sliding glass door that overlooked a small back deck. She went to stand by it, as she felt both the cold and the stale air of the house. In the back yard, the trees were still whipping around, a few small limbs laying here and there on a mown lawn.

"Where did the tree fall?" the man asked.

"Just down the road," she answered. "My mom," – and here she said her name – "is your neighbor." But the man's face showed no sign of recognition, and she realized that of all the stories she'd half listened to over the years, her mother's stories about her neighbors, their semi-monthly wine gatherings on back porches, their shared duties of plant watering and cat sitting, her mother had never mentioned this house, this couple.

She looked beyond the kitchen to a cluttered front room, plastic sheeting on the floor, an easel. She crossed it carefully, pointed out the big picture window. "You can almost see it," she said, angling her neck and pointing.

The man came to stand next to her. He was wearing a worn and dirty t-shirt that hung off his frame over similarly baggy shorts. He had short white socks on with black plastic slides; the plastic shoes made slipping sounds on the plastic sheeting. He stood nearly where she stood, trying to see where she was pointing, at the tree in the road, its wide base upturned, looking like a petticoat, skeletal branches an intricate lace. He was unevenly shaven, the stubble dark and greying, the muscle in his jaw clenching and unclenching. The woman stood a few steps away, looking at nothing in particular, but taking everything in – she was wearing professional clothes: a button-down, dress pants, shoes with a little heel.

"Who's the painter?" she asked, seeing the tubes of what looked like oils, the brushes lined up, but she couldn't smell any of the accompanying smells: no turpentine, or oils. The woman broke into a smile and pointed at the man.

"Oh," she said and smiled at the man but he didn't say anything, didn't look away from the window where he was still craning his neck as if he couldn't see the tree. As if because it wasn't in its usual position, looking recognizable in its tree-ness, it was invisible, wrapped in the black coils of useless and dead power lines. The wind and rain still beating down outside.

"I'm Jeanette, by the way," she said, giving her formal name, the name she used with strangers, at work, in passing. The man introduced himself, and the woman too, but their names disappeared as soon as uttered. This often happened and Jeannie always felt bad about it — it was embarrassing. It seemed like she didn't care or wasn't listening, but really she couldn't remember anything unless she saw it in print, and then she'd never forget it. Years later, she could remember where to find a specific quotation or moment in a book, the orientation on the page, but she'd forget best friends' spouses after she'd met them multiple times unless she wrote the name down and read it.

She heard the woman tell the man that maybe they should open a window for air flow, to even out the pressure in the house. It was getting stuffy, but she remembered this from when she was little, this rule of tornado season, to always crack a window. Jeannie wondered if that was a tornado she'd been driving through on the highway. She started to panic, remembering all the other rules: Don't try to outrun a tornado in your car (but she'd kept driving). Get out of your car and hunker down in a ditch (but the side of the road there was just a steep embankment down to marsh). At least she'd remembered not to drive over the downed lines, and been smart enough to come here, to this stranger's house, and ask for help. To seek safety in the storm.

•

"Hi," she said to the blonde woman who opened the door, "I was trying to get to my mother's − she lives just a few houses down . . ." she paused to push her hair out of her face. "A tree fell across the road," she motioned in the general direction of the tree. "Can I wait out the storm here?"

The woman smiled tautly and held the door as it was, open only enough to let a slant ray of grey light fall across her face. She looked behind her for a minute, looked beyond Jeannie's shoulder at the storm violence, and slowly opened the door. A man stood just behind her in the dated kitchen; she gave him a long look. "Come in."

"Thank you," Jeanie stepped up the cement steps from the garage. Candles flickered on the countertops, augmenting the wan light filtering through a sliding glass door that overlooked a small back deck. She felt the cold of the rain on her skin, realizing she was just wearing her suit, and a transparent cover-up. Gooseflesh rose on her arms and legs. In the back yard, a few small limbs lay here and there on a mown lawn.

"Where did the tree fall?" the man asked.

"Just down the road," she answered. "My mom," – and here she said her name – "is your neighbor." But the man's face showed no sign of recognition, and she realized that of all the stories she'd half listened to over the years about the neighborhood, her mother had never mentioned this couple. Most of the people were her mother's age, retired people, but still active, and they hosted friends, sometimes children and grandchildren, but it was a quiet place to live – no actual young families with children, their plastic play-sets cluttering up the yards.

She looked beyond the kitchen to a cluttered front room, plastic sheeting on the floor, an easel, but no paint-ings in any stages of creation. "You can almost see it," she said, angling her neck and pointing.

The man came to stand next to her. He was wearing a worn and dirty t-shirt that hung off his frame: skin and bones. He stood uncomfortably close. She thought she'd smell body or sweat, just like she thought she'd smell the smells of paint, medium, some chemicals used to clean brushes. But she couldn't smell much of anything. He seemed to be trying to see where she was pointing as he stood there but his eyes were flat and unfocused. The tree lay in the road, its outlines obscured by the rain pounding down.

"When did you lose power?" Jeannie asked, directing the question to the woman, who stood a few steps away, her eyes focused on the man – she was wearing professional clothes: a button-down, dress pants, shoes with a little heel. As the woman flicked her eyes away from the man for a moment, Jeannie took the opportunity to take a step back, away from his closeness, where she could see each individual hair of his stubble.

"Right before you got here," the man answered, moving forward. Jeannie smiled, awkwardly, a wince.

"Who's the painter?" The woman pointed at the man. Jeannie didn't think they were a couple. As she took another look out the window, she realized her car was parked behind another in the driveway, a good ten feet from the open maw of the garage. It must have been the woman's car.

"I'm Jeanette, by the way," she said, giving her formal name. The man introduced himself, and Jeannie repeated it in her head three times, trying to commit it to memory. *Ross Ross Ross.* The woman too, and Jeannie noticed she motioned slightly toward a nametag she was wearing. She hadn't noticed it before, but she stepped forward, crossing back to the kitchen and trying to read the nametag's fine print as she did so. The county's name, some logo. A case worker maybe, or an officer of the court. Not a couple.

She heard the woman tell the man that maybe they should open a window for air flow, to even out the pressure in the house. She heard the woman tell him to "take a deep breath." She heard her say that a few times. The storm did seem to be winding down now, but Jeannie didn't know if she should leave yet, if the road was clear, if she'd be able to get to her mother's, if she'd be able to get back to the highway, back to town. She heard the woman say, "Do you want to call your mother, Ross? To see if she's OK?" She thought the woman gave her a meaningful glance.

Jeannie walked out the open kitchen door into the garage, where the door was stuck open, a result of the power outage. The air was cooler out there, the wind moving everything around. Her cell was in her car.

As she stood at the lip of the garage, Ross called to her, "Where are you going? You're not leaving?" His voice was high-pitched.

"I'm just going to get my cell," Jeannie answered. The wind was still wrestling with the tall pines, big droplets of rain pounding down. She saw the woman cross behind him, say something low. Jeannie ran to her car, grabbed her cell out of the center console. The indicator sounds beeped at her with the door open, her keys still in the ignition. With her head still inside the car, she looked down the road to the fallen tree; up the other way, she couldn't tell if it was clear. She contemplated bringing her tote inside, with her wallet, her things. She left them in the car, sprinted back to the open garage.

She tried calling her mother's landline; the line was dead.

She tried calling her mother's cell, heard her voice for a moment, before the call dropped.

She tried texting her, but the story seemed too long to tell: stopping by unannounced, the tree, at a neighbor's (no, no one she knew). She texted: Are U OK? Storm?

At Library. Why?

She called again, got through. She told her mother the abridged version, and that she likely didn't have power: the tree, the power lines down. When she tried to explain where she was, her mother stopped her. "The gray house?"

"Um, maybe, yeah, I think so . . . like four houses down from you . . ."

"The gray one?"

"Yeah Mom, I think so. I told him your name, he didn't seem to know you . . ."

"Can you get out?" her mother said.

"Yeah, I'm just waiting for the storm . . ." but the cell cut out again.

"Everything OK?" Ross asked. He was standing in the kitchen door.

"Yeah," Jeannie said, "Is your mom OK?"

"Couldn't get through," he said.

"I thought I heard you talking to someone," the woman said.

Jeannie headed back toward the kitchen door, stepped gingerly inside, went to look out the sliding door that faced the back yard. From there, she could just see the road that went the other way, to the highway. She was watching for lights, to see if there was traffic on the highway, if cars were able to get through. She felt someone standing behind her – it was the woman. They both jumped as they heard car doors slam, looked across to the picture window where a truck had pulled up, two men getting out.

"Ross, who is that?" the woman asked, picking her keys up off the counter.

"That's my friend Wayne. Don't know the other guy . . ."

"Ross, you know the rules," the woman's voice was hard, the edges of each word sharp.

"They're probably just checking on me . . . you know, with the storm and all. Not like they could call," and the sky did seem to be lightening, a soft blue breaking through, the kind that's almost green.

"OK, then, well we're going to get going . . ." the woman said, looking at Jeannie, her head motioning toward the open kitchen door, the garage beyond it, the wide open space where the garage door was stuck open, both their cars parked away from the house, near the edge of the driveway, closer to the road than to the house. Jeannie hadn't noticed that before; she did now though, when the man named Wayne, heavy set with a short beard, and the other man, impossibly tall, turned the corner into the garage, both of them in jean shorts and work boots. Because this is probably what happened – the two women trying to leave as the two men arrived. The tall one was in a t-shirt he'd cut the sleeves off himself, the butter-soft side belly pale beneath the edges of ragged fabric. Like the shears were dull. Like he was in a hurry.

Bluebeard's Wife

After the evening events, you've left with a few others and adjourned to the hotel bar. You pull a few of the small round tables together, sit with beers and cocktails and the wet cardboard coasters that have migrated from the bar. Beneath the table, his knee begins to rest against yours and it could be just the close crowding, the jostling of too many bodies ringing the tables. But twice, you lift your eyes, and he meets and holds them for a seconds longer than required, over whatever pint of beer.

You both go out for a cigarette; then another. You small talk about politics, or tomorrow's keynote, or whatever family you've vacated for this small gathering of people like yourselves, your arcane interests, your current projects.

On the third cigarette break, the wind from the small city's riverfront whipping your hair, he says, "I'm thinking of heading to bed." The red lights from the bars and restaurants along the river are slowly extinguishing, their flickers reflecting off the waters' small waves. "I'm thinking you might come with me."

•

The neighbor's house to the north of yours has been vacant for almost eight months. The couple who lived there both moved into assisted living, then the nursing home, then died in close succession. Their son lives in the house to the south of you. This whole block used to be the family's farm, before it was split up into city lots and parceled out. Behind your garage was once the outhouse; you can tell by the towering rings of lilac in spring, lavender and violet and white. When you're up late, wandering between the bedroom and kitchen, drinking water filtered and cooled through refrigerator lines for the way it tastes middle-night, you see all the lights on in the north-side empty house. You stand at the window, watching for the son's silhouetted body. Maybe the lights are on all the time, but you only notice at night. On different nights, different rooms are lit. Maybe there's a system of timers set to switches, an attempt to divert break-ins and petty theft. You watch for hours and never figure it out. Your practical side wonders why all the lights (upstairs and downstairs); wonders about the unnecessarily high electrical bill, wonders who has decided to keep the incandescent vigil going, from room to room to room.

When you can't sleep, you worry about fatal insomnia, the prion disease that affects descendants of particular families, Italians most notably. You've heard that it begins by not sleeping, which results in paranoia, then hallucinations. Progressive, with no cure. From onset, people are usually dead within a couple years. When you were younger, your best friend was Italian, and you were sometimes mistaken for sisters. You have a particular look: dark hair, dark eyes, olive skin, the kind of surname that *could be*. You have a mug that says, "Kiss Me, I'm Italian!" even though you're not. When you were younger, you'd wake up in the middle of the night to find your father sitting on the edge of the bed watching you sleep, or sitting at the dining room table reading old newspapers. *Go back to sleep*, he'd say, and you'd try, lying in bed until the dawn spilled its pink through the curtainless windows in your bedroom.

You can't give blood, per the Red Cross guidelines, and you tell people it is because of another prion disease – Mad Cow. You tell people you were an exchange student in the UK between 1980 and 1996. The truth is that when you were in high school, you'd sew washers into the hems of your jeans to make the weight requirement; you loved giving blood. You'd lie down and watch the thick liquid pink the line and run its slow course between the needle and bag. You'd watch the nurse wipe your inside-elbow with an alcohol pad and flick your green-skinned vein with her finger. You'd watch her sink the needle.

You tell people it's because you spent time in the UK, but that's not really why. You remember the last time you had to leave the reclined, cushioned chair. The nurse had asked if you'd ever taken money, or drugs, or other payment for sex, or had sex with a man who had sex with another man. Or had sex with someone who used needles, or had sex with someone who had ever taken money, or drugs, or other payment for sex. Laughter burbled out of you like fatal air bubbles in the line of an IV. "Who hasn't?" you asked. The Red Cross volunteer looked stricken; then she shook her head a little. She put a brightly-colored sticker on the bag waiting for your blood, and looked away from you to the door, saying low that you could still take a cookie and some juice if you wanted.

•

You are in the hotel elevator with him and when you both go to push the same button, you laugh. Your fingers almost touch. You have had two beers. You think of an article you read recently about men and their behavior around elevator buttons; their compulsive need to push the buttons, to push them confidently, self-assuredly. How if they don't get to push the elevator buttons they make sounds of disappointment and disapproval in the back of their throats. But he doesn't make any of these sounds. In the elevator, the metal interior is slightly blurred with fingerprints, but you can still make out both your outlines as you move moderately, immoderately, toward the floor where you'll both be sleeping. Out the elevator doors, you both turn down the same hallway. He might be following you.

When a man follows a woman – on the street, in a quiet building, a parking garage – there are a number of strategies she can employ, depending on the situation. Whenever you'd travel, when you were younger and single, your uncle used to send you emails with subject lines like "Helpful Travel Tips for Women." They included the requisite pre-planning necessity of mastering karate, but also how to weaponize car keys between the soft crotches of your fingers. Now, the cell phone is the necessary tool – dial 9-1 . . ., activate the record button, pretend to be talking to a friend. Stay alert. To make or not to make eye contact is a decision to be considered on a case-by-case basis – it can either diffuse or escalate a situation. When your uncle was downsizing from house to apartment, he began to apportion his gun collection, and set aside a small pearl-handled revolver for you, reasoning it would fit in your hand, fit in your purse. A lady's gun. It's been a long time since you engaged in any high-risk behaviors, settling instead for watching out of windows, stalking a sleeping house.

At your door, holding only your key card, you realize his room is next to yours and you both laugh, holding eye contact while saying "Goodnight." After you've shut the door, you notice another door along the wall – a door that opens your room into his. You don't believe in signs, but you do believe in desire. You unlock and open this interior door, leave it ajar. You leave your shed clothes in a long trail on the floor, panties stacked on top. You get into the shower and turn it to its hottest setting. Steam escapes over the curtain rod and out into the room where the two double beds sit side-by-side, their coverlets still tidily pulled up. You scrub your skin but leave your hair unwashed. You use the entire bottle of hotel-sized conditioner on the bush between your legs, petting it in the hot shower, making it a pelt of unbearable softness. If he goes to open the door on his side of the room, he won't be able to mistake these signs. These are not bread crumbs, these are hard, shiny stones.

•

You've always thought of "Bluebeard" as a horror story. It's not the blood (specifically described as "clotted" in Perrault's version), or the bodies of her husband's former wives murdered and hung on the walls. It is that after the husband returns comes this sentence: *His wife did all she could to convince him that she was extremely happy about his speedy return.* You can imagine what that entailed: the long night in the bedroom, the honeymoon reenacted with greater and greater feigned pleasure, the forced sighs and sounds. And Bluebeard, being a sadist, would have enjoyed every minute – demanding what he wanted, knowing she'd do each & every act, careful to not betray any moment of hesitation, appearing willing, pliant, excited. You cannot imagine anything worse than feigning to be a willing body taking in another body, to pretend pleasure while hating touch, bile rising in your throat. The way he must have enjoyed her mouth, her everything. There are so many variants of this story, with their own competing levels of gore. But they are all written down by men, finally. Things like a finger chopped off cannot compare to the night not described.

If, in the night, you were to roll over and wrap your arms around his body, would you mistake it for your husband's waiting at home? Roughly the same height and build. Beneath their clothes they might be the same, too – a little paunched around the middle, dark curled chest hair hinting at grey, thin-legged. Maybe you've chosen him because of this: even your fantasies are a disappointment in the end, like thick-lensed glasses that obscure the truth. It would be another disappointment if he touches you the same way your husband does. Maybe all you'll take home from this trip is hotel-sized regret, half-opened and partly used. But you hope he'll ask you what you want, and for the first time in years you'll say it:

Put your fingers in my mouth; I'll put my fingers in yours.

Gather your strength and throw my body around. Don't ask. Pick me up and flip me over. I want to hear the sound of parts of my body hitting headboard, wall, floor.

Make me flail.

Put your mouth all over my body – the unexpected places, back of the knees, tops of the feet where I've collected scars.

Sink your hands into my hair and then coil it until it's a rope of snakes. Pull it down until the sharp chin of my heart-shaped face cants toward the ceiling.

Ask me my safe word. I won't need it, but knowing you asked and that you know it, will make it thrum the air, the base of my spine. The unsaid word will soak the room like storm-humidity, like wind-break trees shirring. No one has ever asked before. My husband doesn't even know I have one. Place it under your tongue like a lozenge that never dissolves. Use your tongue for other things.

•

You're brushing your teeth, the silk robe you brought from home tied loosely. There are sounds coming from the other side of the door. You go and listen, your toothbrush still sideways in your mouth, your hair caught up in a clip. You're wet. You open the door.

THE MONSTROUS-FEMININE

"Kristeva's theory of abjection provides us with an important theoretical framework for analyzing, in the horror film, the representation of THE MONSTROUS-FEMININE, in relation to woman's reproductive and mothering functions. However, abjection by its very nature is ambiguous; it both repels and attracts. Separating out the mother and her universe from the symbolic order is not an easy task – perhaps it is, finally, not even possible."

Barbara Creed

The Monstrous-Feminine: Film, Feminism, Psychoanalysis

Anosmia

You'd been dating for about a year and half and were getting ready to move in together when you found out he was a smoker. At a party with his family and friends, a cousin lit a cigarette, and extended his arm with the pack. A reflex. Quick twitch of his eyes toward you, barely perceptible shake of his head. From across the fire, someone asks: "You finally quit?"

It'd been a cold spring, with summer yet to arrive. Mid-June and only the first bonfire. Someone built up the coals and added a hollowed-out log, arms-length around, so the flames chimneyed up, towering. Crumpled beer cans littered the ground around the pit, dug and formed from a tractor tire. Earlier, there was a string of Christmas bulbs lit up, but the black smoke billowed and obscured the glowing greens and blues of the chemical bursts.

Your lease was going to be up end of the month. The weekend before, he'd showed up with his truck to ferry the big items: your dresser and desk, the bed you'd decided to keep with the newer king-sized mattress and box spring. You were sitting with his friends, these people who had become your people, and learned something new. The fall before you'd gotten a puppy; it had become big enough by then to spend short periods of time outside its crate unaccompanied.

To be fair, you'd never asked and he'd never said anything either way. You'd lost most of your sense of smell as a child, some fever gone high. In the story, your mother told of convulsions, ice in a bathtub and then rushing to the hospital. He did taste of mouthwash often – that must have masked the telltale evidence, mornings when he'd go out to start the truck, and more recently, take the dog out. You've always had to salt and salt and salt to your food to bring out whatever flavor. Next weekend you'll get the last few things from your place – what was your place – and move into his, which is now yours too.

•

Along the ridges are a series of wind turbines, grouped for maximum efficiency. When you drive to the farm, beneath these 'farms,' and the rotor blades are turning, they cast long symmetrical shadows across the road and windshield. When the turbines were first going up, people from the surrounding plots gathered at the township hall to ask questions of the local utility. They'd read online about problems with vertigo, and migraines; had concerns about one of the blades flying off – like some technicolor nightmare from a Metro-Goldwynn-Mayer movie. But after a few years of lower utility bills, things settled down. When you first started driving this route, you'd find yourself slowing and staring, as if the windmills were giant mechanical flowers. They dwarfed the houses and barns and outbuildings, towering above everything human. An edge of shadow moving across your peripheral vision could spook you for a moment.

Now you see things in the periphery all the time – mostly it looks like a mouse, or more properly like the small dark voles that live just outside and burrow in the leaves, or hide beneath whatever you've planted around the foundation. A quick dark scurry crosses the edge of your vision, mostly right side. You've stopped flinching; you know it's a trick of your eyes, something haywire in your retina, a misfire in your brain. But you worry, inside the house, that there may be a mouse sometime, a real one, and you dismiss it. You know you should go to the doctor – find out if you have something worth correcting. Why you're so quick to accept what you see as false.

•

There is some smell here that you can't quite place, and you blame it on your bad nose, but also on familiarity. Like that saying about fish and water. You'll be in the basement, sorting the laundry and think maybe the washer is going. You sink your nose into the wet and washed clothes and try to name the smell (it's not mildew, not mold). But you'll find it in the upstairs bathroom too, in the hall closet, while cooking in the kitchen, even in the back hall where you keep the dog's things: leashes, harness, food and water bowls. The scent permeates. It lingers somewhere in the back of your mind, an olfactory memory that you know as well as you know your own skin. You cannot assign it any language, any label.

You ask him what the water smells like and he looks at you strangely. "Water," he says.

He has night terrors, something you've gotten used to. Those first months, you'd wake in the night to the bed's rhythmic shaking. Or an extended version of myoclonic seizures: arm or leg flail that startled you awake. You'd put your hand on his arm or belly, an attempt to soothe, but he'd stay asleep. Sometimes when the dog sleeps, you watch it dream – its face twitches terribly, low growl, lips pulled back from teeth, and then the legs spiraling like a full-bore run. But he's quiet in bed, bodily-caught in whatever terror, mouth stopped. He wakes sweating and shaking, but won't talk about it. Once you opened your eyes to a rush of air and rolled out of the way as a fist met your pillow. That only happened the one time.

In the shower, you know: blood. Iron-rich water from the well. Even with your terrible nose, you know this smell. You imagine a gathering of women at the township hall, blindfolded, walking in front of a cup of this water from beneath your house, and each would know and name its scent. But only if the men weren't in the room. Women know these things but know men don't want to hear about it. You start buying water in refillable gallon containers, seeing a pink stain on sheets and towels and light-colored clothes, imagining even your cooked pasta has a rouged taint. You use the store-bought water for everything: brushing your teeth, cooking, washing your clothes in the sink. He shakes his head every time he sees you lugging the heavy containers in and out of the trunk of your car but estimates the pennies you spend don't amount to all that much.

You can't remember when you stopped bleeding.

Shedding

The glue traps were a bad idea. They had been hearing scratching in the walls, and thought it was probably mice. They hoped it was just mice. The roof was original, tile, with some damage and likely the entire underlayment needed to be replaced, as well as a significant number of tiles. Plenty of gaps for things to make their way in. They'd wake in the middle of the night and hear the scritch of things behind the mostly-plaster wall, just above the head-board. He could feel his wife awake in the dark next to him, imagine the way she must be looking at him. He promised her he'd take care of it, like he promised her he'd take care of everything when she'd agreed to the house.

It was originally built in the 1930s and was rumored to be a speakeasy. They'd found some interesting things in the attic – things they thought could have been left over from Prohibition. There was a space in the basement that was rumored to have been a tunnel from their house, sitting high on the hill at the top of their neighborhood, to the house across the street. The neighbors in that house had told them about it shortly after they moved in, taken them down into their basement and showed them the door, opened it and pointed to the depression in the earth – told them to look in their own basement for the other end of the tunnel that had been filled in long ago. They'd fallen in love with that story, and the strange copper radiators behind ornate grates in the corner of every room, the arches and coves that distinguished their rooms from every other house they looked at. His wife had agreed to the house because of its charm, and because he promised he could do the updating to the kitchen and bathrooms himself, on weekends, giving her the high-end appliances she wanted, the black and white tiling with glass accents, the rain shower heads and tempered glass sliding doors. She was still waiting.

He hadn't been able to start on any of that yet with all the nuisances that crept up in the first year: the small leaks in the roof; the radiators that burst their seams. Now this infestation in the walls. He chose the glue traps because when he went to select the old-fashioned wood and metal mousetraps – the kind that easily break a mouse's neck when it snaps shut – he heard Melinda suck her breath in, sharply. He could imagine the way the metal-hitting-wood would echo through the darkened rooms in the middle of the night, bouncing off the worn wooden floors from downstairs to upstairs, her body tensing in the bed beside him. He figured with a glue trap nestled inside the bottom cabinets, or better yet, in the basement right outside the door to the defunct tunnel, there would be no noise. He would get up first, and if there was a mouse, and it was still alive, he'd take care of that before she even got up. By the time his wife came downstairs for her coffee, her robe belted around her, their youngest on her hip, the other trailing, all the evidence would be gone. He'd hand her a steaming mug with cream just the way she liked it, and there would be one thing he'd done right.

•

They both woke up to a noise in the kitchen: scraping, and knocking, and clucking, and things moving around. Mel sat straight up. He did too, and she shushed him. He headed down the stairs first, but she was right behind him. The cupboard door was open and a small animal, half-bat/half-rat was skittering around the kitchen floor. Mel screamed. From above, the girls' feet hit the floor and began running from their bedroom. His wife turned toward the stairs, trying to meet the girls before they reached the bottom. Hurried whispering ensued, but he couldn't understand why they were whispering – everyone was up already. Meanwhile, the creature continued its strange hopping, half-attached to the glue trap. Their oldest, Emmy, must have evaded her mother's grasp because she was standing next to him, mesmerized. "It's a squirrel," she said. He looked down at his daughter, calm next to him, watching the frantic creature. She was six.

"It is?" He was still paralyzed, but realized he was holding a wooden spoon as if it was a weapon.

"A flying squirrel." He could see the skin between its foreleg and hind leg, stretched because of how it was stuck to the glue trap. Its small erect ears. Its huge dark eyes. He didn't know how his daughter knew what this thing was – but he knew she was right. Lately, she'd started insisting she was "six and three-quarters" whenever anyone asked.

Melinda had returned to them, holding their younger daughter by the hand. In her baby voice she seemed to be asking about the squirrel, pointing a pudgy finger in its direction. "It's a baby flying squirrel, Lila" Emmy told her, taking her sister's other hand. Melinda looked back and forth between the thing and her daughter. She smiled at Emmy, their smart girl.

"Daddy's going to go set it free," their older daughter started walking her baby sister carefully up the stairs. Melinda looked at him once more, then turned to follow the girls. He heard Lila's slurred baby voice mimic her big sister's, "baba fwyin swirl." He put on his grilling gloves and took the glue-trap-squirrel-package out to the back yard and finished it off with a shovel.

•

The next day, Melinda mentioned that if he was going to dispose of things in the garbage he should probably at least put them in a bag or cover them up. The next night, another baby squirrel showed up in the kitchen. The next night, it was two more. There must have been a nest of them in the walls. This time they weren't stuck to the glue traps, so he had to trap them himself using a blanket and just let them go outside. He called an exterminator to find out what he could do, and when the man came out and climbed up to look at the roof he started laughing. He was relieved Mel wasn't home when that happened. He'd known the roof was in bad shape, but now began to suspect it was more like a sieve, a welcome sign out for all the vermin in the neighborhood, advertising warm walls to get them through the winter. He didn't want to think about the work and money involved in addressing that; he didn't even want to think about how to begin talking to Melinda about it. The exterminator said a litter can vary from one to six if they truly had a nest in the walls – young stay with their mother for up to five months, before becoming independent. Those young he released probably just found their way back. When they'd wake now to a sound in the kitchen, it would be the chirping the girls had started calling "squirrel sounds." The next morning they found the first tooth.

It was an adult molar, yellowed. Melinda took it from Lila's grubby fist while she was sipping her morning coffee.

•

He thought Mel was going to faint when she found that tooth; he'd rushed to calm her down and take it from her and offer some story about how it could have gotten there. It was just a piece of trash, he explained, like a gum wrapper or an old penny. It could have been stuck to one of their shoes or the girls' backpacks as they dragged them up the steeply-slanted driveway from the street. Just a random piece of trash that found its way in. Melinda had always had a thing about teeth. She was sensitive about her own. Growing up, her family hadn't had a lot of money, so going to the dentist wasn't very regular. They couldn't afford braces for the kids, and any repairs were shoddy. She had a crown cap on her front tooth that would come loose every so often. Even though they had good dental insurance now, old habits die hard. He'd once come home to find Emmy and Melinda in the bathroom, his daughter mesmerized

117

watching her mother use superglue to re-attach the cap. Later, he'd reminded her that she could just go in the next day. But she could barely open her mouth to talk or smile with that crooked tooth exposed. Emmy had been looking at her mother as if she was magic.

He found the second tooth in Emmy's "treasure box." She kept her favorite things there – rocks she picked up on the walk to the bus stop in the morning, a perfect pigeon feather from the grocery store parking lot that was laced with iridescent green, a marble scratched to total opacity that had been her grandma's, some whitened sticks from the big lake, a sycamore pod. This one was an incisor. It had a hairline crack down the middle. He pocketed it, hoped she wouldn't notice. When he went up to read the nighttime story, Emmy was pawing around in her treasure box. She set it aside, and listened to the story, quieter than usual, not even jostling for space alongside her sister. He carried Lila to her toddler's bed, tucked her in, and kissed her forehead. He crossed back to Emmy's bed, and went to do the same.

"I'll just get another one, Dad." He froze. The treasure box was still sitting open on the dresser top, the night light's yellow bouncing off its contents. "I know where to get them."

He kissed her forehead and walked out of the room, slowly closing the door.

•

He started with the neighbor across the street, asking a few more questions about the house, its history, the neighborhood. He had two interminable coffee meet-ups, even convinced Melinda to go to the annual block party. They made small talk, and he asked some questions about the house. But he got nowhere. He didn't want Melinda to know why he wanted to know more about the house – as far as she knew, he was just interested in some of their home's unique features. She didn't know anything about the teeth, he was sure. It had just been the one as far as she knew. After he rationalized its appearance in their kitchen, she'd seemed okay, even asked for the strange treasure back – holding it up to the light streaming through the window over the sink. It wasn't that he was trying to keep things from her, but he didn't want to upset her either. He didn't want to feel her awake, staring at him, wondering why they ever bought this house.

The only time in the first months after they'd bought the house that he'd really seen his wife smile was when the first utilities bills for the cold months had held steady, and they'd been able to adjust their budget down. They'd expected a house that old to be inefficient, drafty. But it must have been well-insulated. Maybe some previous owner had done already what they'd planned to do: pull back the rolled insulation in the attic and blow cellulose into every empty space in the walls.

He allowed himself to ask Emmy a few questions. The house gave her the teeth. She could get one a day. They were all different kinds of teeth. She would answer him calmly, holding his gaze the whole time. He said she could keep them, but they couldn't tell Mom. He got a lockbox, and they put the teeth in there, and he'd let her see them, but not touch them. He told her they were dirty, like coins, and would make her wash her hands after she delivered her daily treasure. She wouldn't show him where they came from, and despite searching her room and every inch of the house, he couldn't find any teeth himself. He went down to the courthouse and did a records search and got the name of everyone who ever owned the house. He used his lunch hour to search their names. He didn't know what he was looking for.

Emmy started upping the ante. One night, after they'd read their story and Lila had fallen asleep, she said the house wanted to give her two teeth a day now. She said the house wanted to give Lila teeth too. She said she was having trouble keeping the secret from Mom anymore. He felt panic rising in his throat but he tried to stay calm — they both heard the chirping they'd gotten used to coming from the walls. "Daddy? Can we get a cage for the flying squirrels?" His oldest daughter had an unnerving habit of staring straight at him. "I want to keep them as pets."

•

About a week later, Melinda was drinking her coffee, bent over Emmy whispering something to her. He stopped in the doorway, waited.

"What's going on girls?"

Melinda turned around, smiling. She was wearing her flannel robe, a blue and green plaid, belted tightly. Her hair was still bed-mussed. She looked just like Emmy — or Emmy looked just like her. They had the same dark honey hair, the same pale pink skin, same off-kilter scatter of freckles. In the morning when Melinda drank cup after cup of coffee,

Emmy had taken to mimicking her, sipping her milk from a child's teacup, blowing on it before taking her drinks.

"Emmy has a loose tooth." Next to his wife, Emmy grinned wide, wiggling her front tooth with a pink tongue.

"How much do I get for a tooth?" she asked him. He was probably being too sensitive, keyed on the word tooth. But she said "a tooth," not "my tooth." He started to imagine that this was all a part of it, the collecting of the teeth. His daughter was mercenary. By now, the lockbox was a quarter full, rattling with an assortment of incisors, cuspids, and molars. He kept it in his closet, hidden under a stack of sweaters. He felt it there all the time, as if it was breathing. His daughter had been negotiating with him all along – she had an end in mind. Out on the three-season porch, he could see Lila doing her baby bounce in front of the cage, chanting "Sqwirl! Sqwirl! Sqwirl!" at the cloth pockets where the new pets spent most of the day sleeping. In the evening, with supervision, they'd feed them some fruit, letting them out to roam over their bodies, practicing their leaps from one family member to the next as their skin stretched open to gather air. Melinda would be posed like a scarecrow, holding her arms out from her sides and the small furred things racing from one limb to another and leaping between her and Emmy while Lila squealed. He thought Mel would be squeamish about the squirrels, these wild things in the house, but she'd surprised him by getting the cage herself, and fashioning little fabric pockets to hang inside the bars. She and Emmy would cut up fruit mornings before school, and in the afternoons, feeding the vermin from their hands, getting them used to touch. He'd mostly watch from the doorway. They'd only have them for another month or two before they hit sexual maturity and went crazy for the outside world. He couldn't wait. He hated watching them scrabble all over his wife and daughters, clawing at their clothes and exposed skin.

In all his online searching, he hadn't been able to find any information about the house beyond what his neighbor had told him: the illegal liquor, the escape tunnel that had been filled in. He wondered if there was some connection between the radiators and some sort of still; he wondered about the original owners of the teeth.

He'd taken to sleepless nights, wandering the house listening for creaks of the floor, or feeling for strange currents of air on his face, hoping to find seams in the walls of the house that might show him the source of the teeth. He didn't know how to bargain with his daughter; he knew he was running out of time before he'd have to tell Melinda. The store of teeth in the lockbox grew: half full, nearly three-quarters. Each day she added her new teeth she smiled a secret smile that scared him; missing a front tooth of her own made her look like a jack o'lantern or a harpy. Once, he thought he caught sight of her through the mostly closed door of her room putting one of the teeth into her mouth. He stood very still in the hallway and watched through the slit between the frame and slightly-ajar door. He knew he should go in there and stop her, stop it. But he couldn't. He was afraid of her. He imagined her mouth holding one of those yellowed teeth, alongside her own baby teeth. He couldn't believe in innocence anymore – he found himself rushing through nighttime stories, his bedtime kisses perfunctory. He watched Lila for signs of Emmy-ness.

•

He got an estimate on the roof of almost $70,000; they'd have to take out a loan – he filed it away for a later conversation, not wanting to burden Melinda. He found an artisan who could re-make the radiators, for a price. He held on to this information too, hoping they wouldn't need it too soon. In the meantime, he tried to repair them as best he could. Melinda had loved the way the downstairs bathroom had turned out finally: black and white vintage reproduction tile, clean white fixtures that fit the scale and era of the house. He'd even managed to re-arrange the plumbing to ensure enough space for a corner shower with custom glass walls. It was her favorite bathroom in the house now, but it had taken every spare moment of every weekend of three months. She would kiss him when he came upstairs with drywall cement in his hair.

He'd had to buy a second lockbox once the first one filled. Emmy would make him open the first one to see her horde of teeth before she'd carefully deposit the day's new teeth into the second one. He made sure to obscure his hands on the combination locks when he was spinning the dials. When she washed her hands, she rubbed the tip of her tongue over the new nubs of white growing in her mouth. Watching her rub her soapy hands over each other, working her tongue in her mouth turned his stomach, but he felt like he needed to supervise – to maintain some control over the situation. At the last dentist appointment, the hygienist had called this "eruption" – those little bits of tooth poking up through the gums. Losing the baby teeth was called "shedding." When he looked up, he knew her eyes would be locked on him in the old silvered mirror above the pedestal sink. She'd pantomime an elaborate *shh* motion and run downstairs to the kitchen, where Mel was cutting up fruit. All three of them would feed the squirrels. He'd sit on his bed, head in his hands, listening to their squealing fill the house. He thought the flying squirrels would be long gone by now. They were old enough to be released outside. They had teeth, and claws, and full coats of rough fur. But Mel didn't agree; the play sessions stretched longer and longer now, and he couldn't watch.

When the most recent radiator blew, soaking the wall between the study and the second-floor bathroom, he decided to just hire out the work and begin a big project. He needed some distraction. He cleared the bathroom of all the girls' things. When he moved all the furniture out of the study, readying it for the work crew coming the next day, he was surprised to see a small hole where the wall met the warping wood floors. Behind Melinda's bookshelves. It was crumbly and grubby with dirt, finger stains. He stuck his fingers in and pulled out a tooth, lateral incisor. He scrabbled at the plaster, pulling it away from the wall. Lathe exposed. More teeth. He worked the hole bigger and bigger. The whole wall would be coming down the next day, so he got started early, swinging a hammer erratically across the wall, knocking out pockets of powdery white, splintered wood. More teeth. He went to the basement for the sledgehammer, attacking every spot of wall between the studs.

Teeth poured out, making a sound like sleet. Behind him, he heard laughter.

"Mom always said you would find them," Emmy smiled at him, a sweet and patient smile that looked just like Mel's, when he made another promise about something he'd get to. His daughter ran out of the room, laughter echoing down the hallway. Teeth were still pouring out, a cascade piling on the floor. The plastic clatter of their accumulation sounded like precipitation on a clay tile roof.

Camp Tall Pines

Mindy descended from her cabin, its steps slippery with morning dew. She rested one hand on her belly, while the other held the two-by-four that served as a handrail. She crossed the central path in front of the mess hall, her tennis shoes kicking up the sandy loam where hundreds of small feet would tread the sparse grass and piled moss until it disappeared mid-June. The flagpole was bare, and the only sounds other than waterfowl and peepers were the kitchen staff prepping whatever they'd be serving in about an hour.

In her office, the desk was piled with folders of waivers and emergency contact info for next week's campers; the phone's red dot blinked, and her computer slept. After this week's session ended, she'd be doing her mid-summer performance reviews of the staff, so there was also a stack of handwritten notes waiting to be organized and addressed.

When she accepted the position this past year, she'd looked forward to running her own camp, thought she'd ease into it. Half the staff were experienced holdovers from previous summers; most of the other half were new, but a predictable crop of overeager, shiny college students who'd remembered their years of Girl Scout Camp with ridiculous fondness. And then there were the few who had never been Girl Scouts, but were program staff members with a budget to manage – like the art director, who all had experience in her area, and proved well-prepared for her duties. There were a few international staff members, the cook and his assistant, and two maintenance people.

The returning counselors were her biggest problem so far. Many of them had attended this camp as girls, had been junior counselors, and then aged into paid staff. Anything Mindy changed, small or large, was taken as an assault on their very childhoods. Doing away with the *mandatory* sing-along every night, or changing afternoon swim time by twenty minutes, was met by side-eye and exaggerated sighs. During the summer's three-day orientation, the Waterfront director and Brownies' head counselor had staged an actual coup, marching (like Tencel-shorted pied pipers), out of her afternoon safety discussion, leading all the other staff to the beach, where they'd goaded everyone into jumping in and swimming to the island in the middle of the slow-moving river. They'd said it was "a tradition," as if that explained why Mindy couldn't have been informed beforehand. By the time she maneuvered her five-month pregnant body into one of the row boats waiting in the mud and reeds, and loaded as many lifejackets as she could, the swimmers were half-way across the open water. Mindy didn't care what it was called – she called it an insurance liability.

She had an unlikely ally in her assistant director who was one of the veterans, but seemed to find the members of her cohort mildly annoying at best, and at worst, something to be endured and managed. Mindy at first suspected she was a grown-up *Mean Girl*, but that was her own insecurities showing through. Carmen/Grapevine (they all had camp names, something her returning staff insisted they had to use at all times) was uncommonly beautiful: Nearly six feet tall, lean with summer-browned muscles, and the sort of hair that naturally highlighted and fell into a flattering wavy bob without effort. Grapevine could show up for breakfast in her cutoffs and worn-thin t-shirts, having just rolled out of bed, and even Mindy (who'd never entertained anything other than the most heterosexual of fantasies) stopped for a long minute at the coffee station, watching the steam get caught in her second-in-command's wispy bangs. She would make sure her hands were busy, or she might've reached out and touched Carmen's face.

Carmen seemed to have unending patience for everyone. She'd talk down the returning staff when they'd get riled about some small change Mindy had made; she'd give piggy-back rides to Brownies to distract them when their parents were pulling away too slow, prolonging an already-difficult goodbye, she'd spend extra time with the girls who had trouble fitting in with their campsites' cliques, or whose lips trembled over an unsuccessful campfire or a flipped canoe. Early on, she seemed to bond with the art director, and the international staff, too – the other outsider staff who arrived at camp unsure of their places in the pecking order.

Mindy sorted through the folders on her desk, each tagged with a staff member's name and their camp name. Some made sense – some were just bizarre. The poor girl from England was called "Spots" (British slang for acne). The Russians had names from their country's folklore, and the campers loved those, used them as springboards for stories and to pick up a few phrases over the four-day or week-long sessions they spent at Camp Tall Pines. Many of the other staff had names that echoed the flora and fauna of the area – there was a "Cicada" and a "Tamarack," a "Bluegill" and a "Musky." They named Mindy right away, insisting she have a name fitting her role as camp director. She hated it: House. Maybe they meant she was some kind of foundation, or maybe they meant to describe her dwelling, one of the only house-like structures at camp. But she felt like it was a joke on her size, her waddle, a way of marking her as "other," unlike like the rest of them, who had names that echoed the trees and land they stayed on, the animals and insects that called in the night air. As much as she tried to not let her assigned camp name along with that unscheduled swim bother her, both seemed like hostile acts in the first few days of summer.

She sorted the folders in order: She'd begin with the camp staff who didn't have duties with campers. She'd be able to get their evaluations done over the next few days, before the week ended.

She decided to start with the male staff: the cook and his assistant, the teenaged maintenance help, the assistant to the Trips coordinator, who maintained and catalogued equipment and procured supplies. None of the male staff were allowed close or unsupervised access to the campers, so had very prescribed hours. Mindy would be able to schedule a half-hour with each of them sometime over the next day or two. She could also find time with each of the programming staff members, and Carmen. That would leave a revolving door of counselors for the weekend, and the Trips coordinator, who would arrive back Friday afternoon with her troupe of mosquito-bitten and sunburned girls in tow. This schedule also meant that any anxiety-producing evaluations would be packed into a short timeframe (between Saturday noon and Sunday noon), but over and done with quickly. To compensate for the stress of these sessions, she'd give everyone the Saturday night off. If she was up for it, Mindy would ask Carmen if she wanted to skip out of camp on Saturday night and head into town. They could wear something other than shorts and a Scouting t-shirt, and have a real dinner; they could call each other their given names for a blessed, uninterrupted conversation.

•

Meeting with the cook was fine. He was largely inoffensive, even if his food wasn't. Mindy did ask him, laughing, if he ever noticed that there seemed to be a color-coded scheme to his menus. She could tell by the way he broke off eye contact and the corners of his mouth curled up that he was doing it on purpose. Carmen had recommended Mindy rehire him, as he'd cooked the previous summer, and was looking for work. The first time Mindy saw Carmen and Sam together, she realized theirs was more than a common friendship. Carmen was taller than him, and she had her head inclined so that it almost rested on his shoulder, her long body leaned into his – there was some intimacy there, some palpable comfort.

Sam's eyes cut back to Mindy, who was holding the manila folder, "You noticed?"

Mindy could see how maybe he used to be attractive, but now he seemed tired, old; she knew from his file that he was only in his early 40's. She recognized a familiar wear-and-tear, the broken and healing blood vessels across his nose and cheeks.

"You do it on purpose?"

"I thought it would be funny if the kids noticed . . ." he continued, his hands in his lap were folded over each other, making a pattern of covering each other and holding each other. "What I do is try to go through the rainbow – you know, ROY G. BIV? That almost works over a week."

Mindy noticed for the first time how soft-spoken he was, something sounding broken inside his throat. His hair was dark, almost black, and glossy. Every week he began clean-shaven and, as the week wore on, grew a scrappy beard.

"We're halfway through the summer, a little under bud-get on food . . . maybe we can get some more fresh fruit and veg."

"I was worried about all the extra s'mores stuff I've been handing out," he interrupted. Mindy was worried about this too, but it seemed fine right now. Most nights, there was a steady stream of counselors and kids begging marshmallows and graham crackers from the kitchen's back door. In addition to the regulation chocolate bars, he'd give away peanut butter cups, or peppermint patties for specialty s'mores.

"Can I keep up the colors?"

Mindy thought of how often the orange was cheese sauce, or tater tots, how often the purples and blues were just Kool-Aid. "Sure, keep the colors, but do it more with fresh stuff."

After the meeting, she watched him walk down the path to the men's cabin, about a half-mile from the center of camp. Except for the men's, the cabins were named too, like the campsites. There was an Innisfree, a Shalot – some past director had been a British literature buff. The art director's dog trailed behind Sam. The dog would follow him home during his afternoon break, then follow him back to camp when he returned to begin dinner around four, and the last programming session ended. Somehow, Sam and the dog had formed this affinity, scheduling a mid-afternoon break of quiet away from the bustle of camp, the calling of the children, and in the dog's case, the never-ending reach of the Brownies, always homesick. She heard him make a tongue click at the dog, something she'd heard Pinch, the dog's proper owner, do too, once all the girls learned the dog's name, and there'd been a constant chorus of squealing and calling the dog. The dog became attuned to and learned to respond to that catch-all sound – it meant "come" and "good dog" and "enough."

When Pinch proposed the dog spend the summer at camp, Mindy hadn't been sure that it was a good idea. She'd suggested bringing the dog up for the staff-only weekend to see how it responded to the new environment, the Arts & Crafts cabin, how new people took to the dog. When Pinch unloaded it, a black cocker spaniel, Mindy couldn't help but shiver. As a little girl, her parents had owned a cocker, and it was the meanest fucking dog she'd ever met. By the time they gave it away to a family down the street, it had bitten

Mindy twice. She still had the scars, high on each cheek. Most people probably thought they were acne marks, but it was that dog attacking when she was just a toddler, going for the eyes. She couldn't believe her parents had kept it after the first bite, but they did. The new owners ended up pulling all its teeth because it was so vicious. When she was older, coming home from elementary school, she'd see it in their yard, tied to a tree, toothless and drooling, but barking all the same. Until it died.

The one problem that occurred with the camp dog was during a particularly bad thunderstorm: it got spooked and crashed through the screen door of the art director's cabin. Pinch wasn't home, but the dog had known where to go to find its mistress, which ended up revealing something else Mindy hadn't known about. The dog ran the half-mile to Sam's cabin and they'd been close ever since. Over the first half of the summer, Pinch must have spent a fair amount of time visiting that cabin. Although this wasn't anything Mindy planned on bringing up at Pinch's mid-summer evaluation, she did plan to subtly skirt a few related issues, with an eye toward maintaining camp harmony. Just like the morning after the storm, when she'd found Pinch repairing the screen, having commandeered tools and supplies from maintenance, and Mindy stopped by to mention – obliquely – that camp rules required all regular staff to sleep in their own cabins. The two women avoided eye contact, but passed tools back and forth, saying only what needed to be said and nothing more. Mindy even pet the dog after that.

•

Her meeting with the assistant to the Trips Coordinator was next, and Mindy assumed it would be the easiest one, but she found it to be a strangely awkward conversation. She knew the young man was dating one of the counselors, but they were both college students, and as far as she knew hadn't caused any issues at camp. The girlfriend was one of the most vocal and strident of the returning staff – literally. She'd was only in camp for the first two days each week, and then would lead a group of older girls on a trip to the Porcupine mountains or on the Ice Age Trail, but those two days were full of "impromptu" sing-alongs and campfire stories. Any use of a non-camp name was taken as a personal affront, and any reticence to whole-heartedly join in whatever Cicada deemed the right thing to do was likely to result in a tantrum and the forming of factions. Like clockwork, Cicada would ambush Mindy the first day of each camp week, waiting at the flagpole, with a number of "ideas" and "suggestions" and "brainstorms" that were really just counters to every directive the camp director had made since their last impromptu meeting.

Mindy wasn't sure how the young man in front of her navigated all of this, or what he did the two-thirds of the time his strong-willed girlfriend was out of camp, but he seemed to throw himself into his work. The storage sheds were immaculate, the canoes patched, the shelves of supplies organized and inventoried, everything ready for any of the trips to return and head out at any time. Apparently, sexual frustration was good for job performance. Mindy tried to remember if she ever used to work that hard or be that earnest.

But Mr. Conscientious – she couldn't remember his camp name (it was likely Cicada had picked it for him) – would barely make eye contact throughout the meeting. When she tried small talk – asking him how he was getting along, if he'd found some other staff to be friendly with when Cicada was out of camp – he seemed to physically shut down, the only moving thing to be his bobbing Adam's apple. She tried one last question: "How are things out at the men's cabin?" and he nearly leapt out of his chair, claiming he'd forgotten to make the dry goods run before the Land O'Lakes trip group got back.

Mindy made a note – she'd have to ask Carmen if she had any ideas what was going on. Maybe housing all the men together wasn't a good strategy – maybe there were some issues with such disparate staff, in such different roles and ages, all thrown together, simply because they happen to be the only male staff. Well, not only, there's one more maintenance man, the year-round caretaker (in his 70's), who lived just off camp. Mindy tried briefly to imagine him staying out at the men's cabin, too – maneuvering his slow feet and cane over the threshold, claiming a bunk, storing his hearing aids or teeth in an empty glass, and losing them by morning to either one of the college boys or the cook.

•

Next was the art director. From the beginning, her work was excellent. During the week leading up to camp, she'd done a full cleaning and organizing of the Art & Crafts cabin, a task that had taken nearly two days. Mindy would stop by and see the young woman making huge piles: yarn, wax, paper, crayons, paint, clay. After sorting, she got really meticulous. She tested every marker and pot of paint, discarding or keeping. She took air-dried clay, submerging in buckets and salvaging whatever she could. She subdivided the yarn pile by color and re-rolled into large balls for ease of storage and use. After all of that, she spent another day planning her lessons and activities for the entire summer and presented Mindy with the smallest budget request she'd ever seen. All she needed was fresh clay, paraffin, basic building materials for a hand-made kiln, and sheets from the local Goodwill. Her projects, sorted by age, included using up all the leftover paints with "footpainting" on those old sheets to teach the Brownies about contemporary art, using the broken crayon-bits with the paraffin to make sand candles, and having the older girls follow plans to build an old-fashioned kiln and monitor its temperature to fire their own pinch pots and coiled vessels. That's how she got the name Pinch.

She mostly stayed away from the enthusiastic former Girl Scouts, gravitating toward the international staff, Carmen, and the cook. She and the dog had her own cabin, a lean-to off the back of the nurse's cabin, which ended up working perfectly. On the first night of camp each week, a line of whimpering Brownies with teary eyes would form, complaining of belly aches and sore throats. Pinch would emerge from her back door with the dog, and move up and down the line, squatting down with each girl – most of whom were spending their first night away from home.

The dog would pause and let it itself be held tight, clamped really, its coat collecting snot. It cut the nurse's work in half, cut down on the "emergency" calls made that first night. If there was a particularly bad case, Pinch and the dog would walk back to the campsite with the Brownie and her counselor, sit around the fire for a while, share some marshmallows. The dog was practically a therapy dog.

Mindy met Pinch at the Arts & Crafts cabin; the tables were covered with a thick white film, and the young woman was duly scrubbing the sludge off with a sponge, wringing it out in a bucket. On clothesline strung from the ceiling hung multicolored piñatas, drying in the afternoon breeze.

"Will those be ready by tomorrow?" Mindy asked.

Pinch looked up, startled. Mindy grasped a manila folder in her hand, saw the woman eye it.

"Should be. We made the shells on Tuesday, and they dried first. It's just a thin layer today where we attached the tissue paper." Pinks and yellows and purples, cut in scalloped edges and little frills, fluttered above the tables, in the little wind coming throw the screen walls.

"They did all that today?"

"Well, I precut most of the tissue paper," she motioned along the long counter, where there was still strips of precut paper, sorted by color, were assembled for the girls to choose from to create patterns. "I left some for them to cut so they could learn how to do it, but then they could just attach whatever they wanted." She scrubbed at a hardened clump of white on the table. "I figured it would be something cool for them to take home from camp."

"Is that all glue?" Mindy motioned at the tables, a mess of white wet quickly drying.

"It's old fashioned glue. Got some flour from the kitchen. When I was little we had an exchange student from Mexico, and she showed us how to make piñatas like this."

"You do a great job with this stuff," Mindy said.

Pinch straightened up, "Thanks. Time for our review?"

"Yup."

"I'm ready for a break anyway," and she moved to the first table, already cleaned.

They had some things to talk about but Mindy started with all the good: she had no complaints about Pinch's work, or the projects she did with the girls; her time management, her budget, and her recycling of the leftover materials was amazing. Halfway through, she sighed, "Can I call you Leila?"

"Please – I hate 'Pinch,'" the young woman smiled ruefully.

"I hate 'House,' please call me Mindy," she matched her smile. "If you don't like it, why'd you go with it?"

"Oh, you know, they get so excited when they come up with a name . . . and it's not like I really care, but, it's not my name, and 'Pinch' like a pinch-pot, it sounds like a fat joke," Leila laughed, but it had an underbelly of anger. It was funny to Mindy that that's exactly how she felt about her name.

"So, Leila, we do have something to talk about . . ." Mindy continued.

"OK."

"I know that most nights, you leave camp . . ."

"Uh huh," Leila was leaning forward a little, picking at her hands where there was still flour-glue stuck in her cuticles, under her nails.

"So, this might not have been clear to you, not having worked at a camp before, but those aren't really your nights off," Mindy looked directly at her. She suspected the young woman had no idea that even though she didn't have campers to supervise in the evening, once dinner and final flagpole activities were done, she still wasn't free to do whatever she wanted. The cook and the maintenance staff were, but they were employed by the camp facility, not the Girl Scouts. The Girl Scouts counselors and programming staff only had one night off per camp week. She explained all this to Leila and watched her listen.

"We've been going up to the dam, not into town or anything . . ." it was an awkward excuse and it didn't really matter. Off camp was off camp. Off camp meant they could drink or smoke or do whatever. The dam was a favorite place to swim, or jump from the small county bridge into the water, where the rushing water scooped out a deep ravine in the sandy bottom of the otherwise shallow river.

"I know you've been joining Marja or Schuka on their nights off, but that's their one night – you only get one night per week. You can pick a night, but the other nights, you need to stay on camp," Mindy reiterated her main point. She didn't want Leila to explain what she'd been doing and she didn't need any details. She simply wanted to clarify, moving forward, what Leila should not be doing.

"Oh," Leila paused. "What should I be doing?"

"That's up to you – you're really helpful the first night of camp, you and your dog," and as if on cue, she saw the spaniel coming down the path from the direction of the camp mess. "Maybe you can find something like that? Visit one of the campsites? Or check in with Grapevine," she thought she saw the girl draw back a little, "see if she needs help with anything?"

"Sure, Hou – er, Mindy, I'm sorry. I really didn't know."

"I figured. Don't worry about it," Mindy stood up, stretched a little and leaned backwards, letting the muscles of her back lengthen before they went back to doing the work of supporting her and her pregnancy for a few more hours. "Oh," and she tried to flash the young woman what she hoped was a conspiratorial smile, "don't go visiting the men's cabin, even though that's technically on-camp." But at this, Leila didn't react at all.

•

The rest of the meetings went largely as Mindy expected. Some were fine, and a few were awful. A few of the most hostile returning staff decided to take it upon themselves to turn their evaluations into an evaluation of their new camp director. Most of these, Mindy ended the same way – with a prepared statement. *She was the director, they were her employees, and the employees of the Girl Scouts Council. They should all try to work together and get along for the rest of the summer, ensuring the best possible experience for their campers. After all, that's what this was about: the girls. Things were changing in Girl Scouts, and they all had to adapt – nothing was ever going to stay the way it was, the way they remembered camp from when they were younger.* Although

Mindy didn't say this, in the end, she was the one with the power. If they couldn't do the job they were hired for, and do it to her satisfaction, they wouldn't be hired back. Initial feedback from the families and campers already was overwhelmingly positive. The Council was happy with a number of the changes she made and had already offered her a contract for next year.

She was also happy that Grapevine accepted her offer for Saturday night out, and even happier when she agreed to the "No camp names!" suggestion. She looked forward to getting to know Carmen better, finding out about her history with Camp Tall Pines and what kept her coming back. She was also interested in knowing if she wanted to return for the next summer. Carmen even suggested a restaurant, a place Mindy remembered from earlier in the summer when she and Brad had driven past it and thought they'd want to stop back in. A nice Northwood's restaurant, upriver from the dam, with a long dining room overlooking the reservoir. Nestled between two towns, the restaurant was moderately busy when they arrived, so Mindy was glad she'd called ahead. It didn't take long after they were seated for the stories to start. Although she'd been around women all summer, there was something different about the easy camaraderie with Carmen. When she thought about it, Mindy realized they probably weren't that far apart in age – maybe ten years? Before she could think much more, Carmen just asked.

"I'm thirty-four," Mindy answered, her hands drifting down to rest on her belly. Carmen's eyes followed her hands. "This is our second."

"I'm twenty-six," she volunteered. "Do you miss your family?"

"My husband and son will be coming up next weekend and staying through the week," she smiled. "I think they maybe miss me more than I miss them . . . wait, don't tell them I said that." Mindy was drinking a 7-Up, but had asked for added cherries, so it would feel festive. "My husband, Brad, is a great father."

"Oh, so . . ."

"So I kind of like being on my own." Mindy finished the younger woman's thought, assuming that's what she was asking.

Carmen was heading to graduate school in the fall, leaving the Midwest and moving to Delaware to start a master's in social work. She could barely wait, but was trying to not convey her impatience too strongly to her close-knit family. She'd be the first one to move out of state, and her family worried. They wondered why she was going back to school; worried about her living out East, about what she was going to do with that degree. Mostly they worried what her life was going to be like since it had become clearer to them that she truly wasn't going to be dating a man, or marrying one anytime soon. She'd come out to them in college, and they'd ignored if for a few years, continuing to casually suggest they knew nice single men, bemoaning that she'd never have children or a family. So, she just kept coming out, over and over again, until it seemed to take. When the Supreme Court finally handed down their Obergefell v. Hodges decision, she got her mother a *Congratulations!* card.

Inside, she wrote: "Someday, I'll be getting married and having a family! Love you."

Carmen had returned to camp this past summer because she knew why their last Director had quit: It was in protest over the Girl Scouts' position to support trans girls. She didn't know how many others of the returning staff knew about this. She tried to bring it up with a few, the few who she thought would be sympathetic with the queer community, or who might have some affinities, or who were slightly more liberal. But it seemed like every conversation she initiated would circle back to whether they were singing the fucking Christopher Robin song regularly enough, and eventually Carmen just gave up. So, she gravitated toward the new staff, the international staff, the new Director (who knew the story), and Sam.

She'd met Sam at an AA meeting a few years ago. He was five-years sober; she was working on two. She'd gotten him the job at camp the first summer, and vouched for him this year too. Last summer, they'd spent many evenings together, the whole season a deeper detox – from their families, from cities, from so-called friends who never really supported their sobriety, from the light pollution of even smallish cities. They'd do a daily reading or affirmation, and in the evening, sit with toes dipped into the quiet lake (really just a widening of the river) and silently be there for each other in a kind of mutually-partnered sponsorship. Sam had been sober longer, but he'd also been more beaten down by life. Carmen didn't think her family had any idea how much she self-soothed, or how much of that self-soothing was chemical. When they pretended not

144

to acknowledge who she really was, they also shut down some avenue of communication and love that she thought would never not be there. People like Sam, and her sponsor, became the people she turned to. This summer, she felt like she lost Sam.

It was Leila. Carmen didn't know what was going on, but she knew that Leila had been spending too much time with Sam, and that likely, alcohol had been involved. She'd tried to talk to Sam about it a few times, but he just smiled his crinkly-eye smile and waved her off. And while Sam and Leila certainly weren't a couple, the dog's behavior made it clear that it was comfortable going from his cabin to hers. But as angry as Carmen was about that, she also worried about Leila.

Carmen had run into her at the dam one night. Leila, clearly drunk, was a souped-up version of her daytime self. Carmen had seen her manage twenty Brownies with tiny shovels and pots of hot wax, corralling them into making multi-layered sand candles with triple-wicks, and no one ended up with burns, hurt feelings, or misshapen projects. She had energy, skills and an aggressive speaking voice. Drunk, she had energy and aggression. Carmen hadn't been meaning to stay by the dam anyway; hanging with drunk people wasn't her thing, but she was a little worried about the way they were jumping off the bridge, not even waiting until they were safely in the middle. Carmen remembered the pleasures of jumping off that bridge – the rush of leaping off the concrete, the jolt of hitting the water's surface. She knew too that after going again and again, not even feeling a brush of sand with the tips of toes as the body throttles down, a person gets braver, more reckless, and jumping closer to the sides becomes part of the thrill. So while the Russians were by the fire, and Leila was fumbling for her keys, Carmen tried to slow her down, offered them all a ride back to camp.

Leila came at her, her smile wide and drink sloppy, her eyes dilated and glittery in the moonlight. She leaned her full weight against Carmen, pining her against the car. Before she could move away, or even tell her to back off, she felt the younger woman's hand on the inside of her right thigh. Carmen froze — she hadn't expected this. She didn't know whether that was because she'd assumed Leila was straight, or because she wasn't really out at camp. Caught in that moment of indecision, when she couldn't quite decide how to say no (even though no is exactly what she wanted to say) — she felt Leila's hand move. First, it was the slightest move of her finger — the ring finger maybe? The pinky? Then Leila's entire hand moved up Carmen's thigh, crossing the border of her shorts. Carmen tensed, but Leila wasn't looking at her — she was looking past her somehow, beyond her, but tuned in to her body, to what she was doing with her hand.

Then Carmen remembered her size, her strength. She pushed the younger woman away, not caring that she fell to the ground, not caring that she was drunk and shouldn't be driving, not caring that maybe they'd all stay and drink more, and continue to jump into the river, risking their soft bodies against the dangerously-shifting currents. Carmen got in her car and drove back to camp.

146

•

"Carmen? . . . Carmen –?" Mindy interrupted her memories. The Camp Director had drained her tub of sparkling soda, was chewing on a cherry stem.

"Oh, sorry," Carmen tried to recover, "you were . . ."

Mindy looked confused, but picked up the conversational thread. "I was just saying that I talked to Leila about the night off issue. I don't think it'll be a problem anymore."

"Oh, that's good," Carmen took a deep breath, took a sip of her Coke.

"So, I was thinking she's someone I'd invite back for next year."

"Um . . ." Carmen paused, "I wouldn't." Mindy leaned forward, the corners of her mouth turning down. She shook the bit of ice left in her empty tumbler, signaling the waiter.

In her head, Carmen was running through all the reasons she couldn't give to back up why she'd say this. She couldn't talk about Sam and AA, and the way she worried that Leila was threatening his hard-won sobriety. She couldn't call Leila a slut, that wasn't fair. She couldn't tell Mindy about what happened at the dam – out herself, and maybe Leila, and make an accusation of – *what?* – pushiness? a drunken fumble? What would she call that? Carmen remembered again the long moment it took for her body and mind to connect, to realize that what Leila was doing wasn't something she had to numb herself to, wasn't something she was going to acquiesce to, or allow.

"She's sleeping with the assistant to the Trips coordinator." This was true; A few days ago, Carmen had walked in on them in the dry goods pantry.

"What?" Mindy swallowed the half-chewed bread roll in her mouth, dropped her butter knife with a clatter. "Are you sure?" she half-mouthed, half-whispered.

"Yup. Caught them."

"Oh."

"Not that there's a rule against that or anything but . . ."

"Wait, aren't he and . . ." Mindy struggled to pick up the thread of her thought, remember the girl's real name "practically engaged? . . . Promised before God, or something?" One of things Cicada was always on her about was the pre-meal prayers, the evening "reflections," the choice of camp songs . . . this year Mindy had made an effort to include poems, inspirational quotations, and prayers from all sorts of different religious traditions. Cicada had a problem with this. The last thing Mindy would have thought Cicada would have had a problem with was her boyfriend/ fiancé, who seemed as publicly committed to her as she was to him.

"Things are going to get pretty awkward the second half of camp," Carmen shrugged.

•

Driving back to camp, they turned in the back gate, which skirted the maintenance cabins, the service access road, and the small staff parking lot, which was mostly empty. Mindy stopped and Carmen got out, taking the path to the men's cabin. The moon was a waning gibbous, and between the starlight and the moon's light reflecting off the thin aspens and paper birches, there was enough light to not trip over tree roots, or moss and lichen-covered small stones that humped up out of the ground. The men's cabin was set up on a small hill, and the lights were on. There were at least two bodies moving around inside, casting shadows. Carmen figured she'd find what she'd find.

Mindy continued on slowly. A narrow road cut through the center of camp directly to her cabin – a small perk, but Mindy was thankful for it this summer. Halfway through and this pregnancy was easier than the last, or maybe she just knew what to expect this time. By lunchtime, she'd feel a wide band of tiredness in her lower back, a settling, to her legs. After checking in with counselors and campers at the midday meal, she'd return to her cabin and lie down for a few hours, try to nap a little, or do some easy work on her iPad, return some calls. She was looking forward to seeing Brad and her boy next week.

She trusted Carmen's opinion of Leila, knew to listen to her, to listen to the growing, gnawing worry inside her. The close-knit community of camp was its own ecosystem, and now she was hyperaware of the way it could be – would be – set off. If Cicada found out about whatever was going on between Leila and the Trips assistant. If some sort of competition or territorial dispute broke out in the men's cabin, between two of Leila's conquests. But there was something else too, something Mindy couldn't quite figure out. Maybe it was the way Leila didn't really seem to try to cover, or mind if her extra-curricular activities were public or not – she only seemed to mind if they interfered with the perception of how she did her job. Or maybe they were a part of how she did her job: it all seemed interconnected, her ability to make things happen, to manage resources and people.

Maybe it was that Mindy kind of appreciated Leila's difference from the other staff. She was slow to join scripted activities, was less of a do-gooder, with fewer obsequious smiles, and was less concerned with appearances. She was always a little unkempt – half her clothes were hand-made or ill-fitting, but in a way that seemed a little sly. Her hair was often snarled and tousled, slick with its own natural oils, and pinned up with clips or bobby pins, sometimes just a smooth-whittled stick stuck through a messy bun. But, if Mindy was honest with herself, it was that the younger woman reminded her of some version of herself.

She and Brad had dated on and off throughout college, but Mindy always kept a barrier between them, usually seeing someone else on the side. She was meticulously honest about this with Brad, and whoever else she was seeing, or hooking up with. Brad had always wanted a family, wanted to get married, wanted the whole fantasy of what that would be. It's why Mindy would never let herself get too serious about him – they wanted such different things. So he'd date someone else, someone more suitable. Or she would.

Mindy would stop by his place after months of not seeing him, and he'd answer the door like he was expecting her all along, just turn around and leave the door open wide for her to follow him in. Or he'd call when she was dating someone else, and they'd talk for hours, and it would be like there wasn't anyone else anyway, never had been; their voices two whispers on the phone saying impossibly intimate things about what their bodies missed, what they wanted to do to each other. That Brad turned her on: percussives out of the dark softening to syrup-voiced vowels. She could hear his needs through the phone; she could answer it.

A couple years after college, they finally had it out. He offered that if she would marry him, be up for having kids, he would stay home with them and she wouldn't have to. True to his word, once she and their son came home from the hospital, he left his job and took over the infant care: the waking up all night long, the diaper changing and feeding. As soon as she was feeling up to it, Mindy went right back to work. Brad became the stay-at-home dad, the manager of play dates and daycare searches. Pretty soon, he'd start all over again. All over again, he'd be playing defense with both their families, his friends, the other mothers who didn't understand why Mindy wasn't there.

Mindy had been Brad's first – she'd pursued this shy sweet guy until she got what she wanted. What she wanted was to see who he really was. Beneath his physically-imposing 6'4" exterior, his large hands and gentle eyes, she wondered what it would be like if he could hold her eye contact for as long as she wanted him to. After their first date, when she brought him back to her parents' empty house, she'd stood still and close to him in the kitchen, looking up at him across the foot and a half height differential, daring him to break eye contact. When he didn't, she'd moved in closer. Since then, his body had always been home to her, a home she reveled in being able to leave.

151

•

Over the next week, everyone would tell their stories.

Carmen's arrival at the men's cabin precipitated the assistant to the Trips Coordinator leaving, but he'd looked to be on his way out already. Leila's dog was next to Sam on his bed, but Leila wasn't. Carmen and Sam stayed up talking all night. If Carmen had been asked to describe the mood when she arrived, she would have said it reminded her of a cold campfire – the smell in the morning of ashes extinguished by time, maybe a heavy dew. But no one asked her to describe that; no one thought she or Sam had anything to do with what happened. For a time, it seemed like maybe they were the last people to pinpoint the missing man's whereabouts – the last sober people anyway.

She and Sam had it out, sort of, the way two friends who have seen each other bare it all before rooms of strangers, can bare it all in smaller rooms: a different kind of intimacy. They held each other, for the ways they were both broken and both hopeful. Sam explained that waking up one night to whispers, he'd seen Leila in the bunk across the room straddling the boy, and that had soured him on her – but he wasn't going to hold that against the dog. Sam and Carmen and the dog all slept in the same bed that night. Leila stopped outside the door in the morning, clucking her tongue to retrieve her dog, but she didn't come inside.

He wasn't really a boy, anyway, the assistant to the Trips Coordinator, even if he seemed that way to Sam. He wasn't old enough to drink, and rarely did, but he'd joined the rest of them on that Saturday night. Well, most of them – the counselors, the international staff, Leila – but not Cicada. It was a Saturday, midsummer, and they had the night free. That's why the lot had been empty when Carmen and Mindy got home from their off-camp dinner. The staff had gone to their different places – some into town for a bite, or to a local bar – but most ended up at the dam late. A bonfire, bottles, some weed, maybe pills. The dark of the woods and no children to care for, even fewer rules to follow.

Cicada and her almost-fiancé had argued, but about what she hadn't been sure. He'd left and gone to join the others. When she couldn't find him the next morning, getting coffee or juice or toast, she asked the English girl Spots, but she said she hadn't seen him. When he wasn't there for lunch, she asked the cook, but he hadn't seen him since the night before. She worked up her courage to approach Grapevine, leaning over the railing of the kitchen's back porch, a steaming mug in her hands. Grapevine said she'd last seen him when he was leaving the men's cabin the night before. Grapevine had looked tired, unbeautiful – shadows greening under her eyes, and her hands shaking a little.

Cicada tried not to raise her eyebrows at this, not to let her disappointment show. So Grapevine was at the men's cabin. She'd better report this to House. Now she had two reasons to talk to her, and it was only Sunday, less than a day since their last meeting.

•

By Monday, and one of her staff still unaccounted for, Mindy filed a missing person's report. The local sheriff came out to camp, and interviewed everyone who had seen the young man in the twenty-four hours before his disappearance, now known to be sometime late Saturday night or early Sunday morning.

Mindy wondered if she shouldn't have given everyone a night off together, if she'd made a mistake. She wondered if, when she and Carmen were eating dinner, looking out the dining room window, if the gathering was already forming downstream at the dam, and her staff were doing whatever they were doing that led to one of them going missing. Maybe that had been the gnawing feeling in her stomach she'd tried to fill by eating roll after roll from the bread basket on the table, pretending her soda with a cherry was a cocktail. For the first time, she felt bad for Cicada, whose face slackened and set a little more each day; she sent Carmen on the Porcupine Mountains trip, tried to handle every request of her difficult employee with kindness. She counted the days until Brad came to camp.

She hoped and hoped that the assistant to the Trips Coordinator had run off, left, afraid that he'd be found out. She hoped he was mostly OK somewhere.

•

His parents came up, then left. There was nothing for them to do. Cicada went back to her work, less enthusiastic. The sheriff stopped back and questioned everybody who'd been at the dam one more time; there was talk of dredging the river. There had been no activity on his credit cards. No one had heard from him. One quiet evening, Mindy left camp, wedging herself into her car, her belly butted up against the steering wheel, and drove the back way to the dam – the camp access road to the single lane county trunk, then rolling over the gravel crunch on the far side. The grass was beaten down from the haphazard parking of cars and in the border of poison ivy and bent over milkweed and chicory, dulled bottoms of aluminum cans glinted. She could see the remains of a fire pit, whitened wood and ash soaked by the previous night's rain.

Mindy walked out to the center of the bridge where it spanned the water, and leaned over the railing, trying to imagine the last night anyone had seen Colin. Half memory, half fantasy. Young people goading each other to be more reckless, more carefree. She felt so old, the way her lower back pained, the way she leaned backwards, her hands splayed low behind her where her back met her ass, the pressure relieving for a moment the dull ache that greeted her each day. She could see them, each jumping closer and closer to the sides of the river where the concrete barely cleared the packed dirt of the bank. Someone passes a bottle. Liquid brown as the stream water. Lights spark and flicker: cigarettes and bowls and a firefly here and there by the bank. Maybe someone like Leila grabs him and kisses him, her mouth sweet, burning with whatever liquid. Maybe Colin's showing off, angry from the fight with Cicada, or dreading going back to the cabin he shares with the cook, or maybe he's just young and not thinking or feeling anything. Mindy remembers this, she knows this – she grips the thin metal of the guard rail, steps up so her sneaker-clad feet are balanced on the first rung. She can feel its sharp edges cutting into and through her shoes, pressing into her arches, one more place she's sore. The aluminum presses cold against the underside of her belly, where her pregnancy will drop as the summer wears on. Her navel has just popped out, and it catches against the metal of the safety device.

She looks down at the white froth on the water, thinks about Colin jumping. The water catches him, bracing cold. On the shore, there is laughter. All around him, laughter, as his head breaches the surface, then goes back under. From the narrow below the dam, the river widens into shallows, bordered with reeds and cattails, waterlogged trunks and branches caught up. In the moonlight, something might have broken the silvered surface now and again, twisting, moving quickly then catching against a rock, then breaking free.

Sunday Dinner: A Fable

On the front lawn, the deer has been hobbled. Tied. Blood bubbles from its wide black nostrils – its antlers are little nubs, worn of their new velvet, with bits and strips hanging. Because captive deer are dangerous, there is a roped perimeter around the animal, thick cord tied tree to tree to keep the children a safe distance, and they do. The older boys are there, watching the younger children, and the dogs lie down their own respective distances away, watching the animal struggle – its furious sharp hooves, as it is caught on its side or its back, its eyes wide with fear and shock. The neighborhood gathers for this Saturday morning show.

In the house, you watch out the big front window, gathering what you want to say. Your brother is there, and the deer is his. Tomorrow, you will eat it. You all will. It had been announced before this weekend, that he would be bringing the meal. He arrived with his wife and children, their dogs, and the deer. You had not known he'd meant the deer. You remembered when he'd posted the photo of the fawn last summer, spotted still, abandoned. Then more photos: the fawn and the dogs in the yard, settled already into an unlikely pack. The kids taking turns bottle-feeding when it was its smallest. The pallet on the screened-in porch, then the out building and large pen, the field that became its unlikely home. Looking out the window, it doesn't make any sense – that the pet deer has become meat.

Sense isn't being made in any room of the house either, in any space sunlight hits. The kitchen brims with your mother and sister-in-law, companionably chopping vegetables for sides and salads, children running in and underfoot, reporting on what's transpiring on the front lawn, still calling the deer by its name. Your brother and father are in the backyard, digging a roasting pit. You keep rushing to the bathroom to vomit, but instead look at yourself in the mirror, listening through the narrow window to the chorus of children's voices from the front yard. A crowd is forming. The deer beats and beats itself bloody; the lawn becomes a sandy-loamed circle of dirt, wet with saliva and blood and urine, the children glued to the spectacle.

You go to your brother – your brother who you love, who has always been so logical, and kind – and tell him this is wrong, that he should kill it already, it is suffering. You say you'll do it and imagine the weight of the gun in your hand. You look down at your hand, trying to see the gun there: the dark handle and delicate barrel, the heaviness, the small engraved numbers. The gun that is not there spans your thumb apart from your fingers and you'll need your other hand to open the cylinder and load it; you'll need both hands to hold and aim it.

You've only shot a handgun once, and it's been a long time since you've shot any gun. Even when you did, it was mostly target practice: beer cans, clay pigeons, or paper targets tacked to trees. But you were a good shot, you remember that. You'd have to get close to the deer and they're

158

dangerous – they jump and kick, with impossibly sharp hooves, they bite and head butt. You imagine the down-soft fur between its eyes like some loved pet, the way its eyelids would be translucent over convex eyes, and the eyelashes.

You remember the eyelashes from the twin fawns taken from the gutted side of the roadkill doe hung in the garage when you were little. How impossibly long the lashes, how black, and the slight curl on the edges. Girlish, you think now. Beautiful, you'd thought then. How the few men you'd seen with lashes like that have undone you, how when they begin to cry their eyes widen and fill, and the eyelashes jump into hyper relief. You'd seen your brother cry once, long ago. Now, when you say you'll do it, he just looks at you. You think you see a smirk. He looks long to the front yard then goes back to his digging.

You know you couldn't do it. And you don't want to. You didn't take the deer in, didn't care for it – show it some kind of love. You didn't find the small spotted thing, all soft ribs & call it yours. Your brother doesn't stop his digging, but you hear him: *This is how it has to be.*

•

If this is how it has to be, this is how it'll be. You walk out front and sit down on the ground with your nieces and nephews, the neighbor's children, the children from the next street, even the older kids you usually watch with trepidation as they bike by mid-summer, loud and shirtless, sitting back on the seats of their bikes, riding no-hands, and already moving lanky into the spaces of adulthood, slaloming their curves until you honk softly, waiting for them to move out of the road. They are here too, quiet, and you are joining their circle – the circle around the deer thrashing in pain.

Maybe all those photos you saw were some kind of myth-making, some crafted story, only part of the truth. Maybe once the fawn lost its spots and didn't take the bottle anymore, it was moved to the out building to keep the kids safe. You remember bruising on your niece's arm; for a few months there, she seemed "accident-prone," a pattern of blues and greens and faded yellows. A season of flinch. You remember how the kids never talked about the deer after that first summer. Some animals aren't pets and never should be. Some animals look sweet when they're new, small and scared, but are always animals, teeth and hooves. And maybe those pictures of the deer and dogs in the backyard were prey and pack – you scroll back through your phone and notice the deer always at the ragged edge of the lawn, the dogs with their heads low and a raised band of fur at the withers. Those same dogs in the circle now, watchful and panting, but not relaxed, not yet.

The deer and the dogs lock eyes sometimes. The deer spasms and a collective sound goes up from the gathering, something you cannot fully describe, or do not want to. The shovel-and-earth music from the backyard has quieted, one more job done.

The meat will be delicious, you know. Your brother is a good cook, a good provider, heavy with the salt. You will hold the pit-braised flesh of the deer between your teeth tomorrow and note its tenderness. Dusk is coming on.

Treasure Hunt

She'd begun the night before, after the boy had gone to bed. Her husband was watching TV, his feet up on the coffee table, the blue light bathing his face. The first few times she just stepped over his outstretched legs, but the fourth time, he reached forward and wrapped his arms around her slight form. She was holding a skein of rainbow-colored yarn loosely, letting the lengths unfold themselves and stretch from here to there. Already there were knots and gathers. For the next batch, she thought, she'd probably re-roll it first into tight little balls. Or maybe she'd roll it onto the leftover cardboard tubes she'd been saving for some future project – then she could put the roll over a dowel or larger knitting needle and make fast work all over the house. She was so deep in thought about how best to spiderweb all the rooms that she didn't even notice that her husband was holding her, immobile.

"Carol," he interrupted her thought, "what are you doing?"

"Oh." She looked down at the limp yarn in her hands. It was a cheap poly, and the edges frayed and caught in her thinned nails, stray fibers grabbing each crack and crevice. "Working on the party."

"Already?"

161

"Yes, I'm getting started tonight," she said. She tried to explain the maze, the Treasure Hunt – how the whole house would be a web of yarn, and each child would have their own trail to follow to treasures, small and large, leading to their big surprise. Midway through her explanation, he turned his attention back to the TV.

"I'll probably be up late tonight," she finished, cutting off her explanation. In this case, like so many others, she wasn't able to communicate her excitement, her careful planning, the way she hoped the children's faces would light up when they saw it.

"Matt?" she called him back to her.

"Yeah?"

"In the morning, I want you to take him out for breakfast – a big breakfast. Pancakes and syrup."

"OK."

"That way, if you bring him back around eleven, everything will be all ready and the other children will be arriving."

"OK." She left him there, with whatever he was watching, and went back to her preparations.

•

In the morning, Matt woke and the spot next to him hadn't been slept in. When he went into the hallway, light filtered through the high transom window and caught the feathered yarn that blocked the stairs to the living room, to the basement. The hallway was mostly clear, and he woke the boy, told him to get ready for breakfast. They brushed their teeth together in the shared bathroom, washed their faces and dressed. Somewhere in the house, Carol was moving. The boy was excited for his birthday party, anticipation already building in his small-boned body.

As they were passing through the kitchen, the boy caught sight of strings of yarn peeking from the living room, stretched across the length of the open spaces. He opened his mouth in a wide O. Carol met them at the door, caught the boy up in her thin arms.

"It's a surprise for your party," she said, holding the boy. The freckles on his face matched the freckles on his mother's, orange dots in butter cream. "Don't tell anyone," she cautioned, smiling wide.

The boy grinned back showing gums, promised by pursing his lips and sealing them with his hand and fingers pantomiming a key and lock. They both laughed. Matt put his hand behind his wife's head.

"Were you up all night?" She nodded. She was paler than usual, a little flushed. "Promise me you'll eat something," and she nodded again, broke eye contact. His eyes swept the kitchen: the table covered with hanks of yarn, scissors, tape, paper, twine and glue. Hammers. Rope. The coffee maker's indicator light on, a pot of thickened liquid. "Besides coffee," he said, looking meaningfully at her. She nodded again. Carol kissed her son on his nose; she kissed Matt on his lips. Her breath smelled sweet and chemical.

•

When Matt and the boy arrived back at the house, shirts syrup stained, there were a few cars there already. Children and parents were milling in the backyard. It was a beautiful late spring Saturday. Balloons in green, yellow, purple, orange and blue were tied in the trees that ringed the small backyard. On the picnic table was a self-serve punch dispenser, a veggie tray, a fruit tray, and a note from Carol.

Welcome to Cade's 8ᵗʰ Birthday Party!
Please grab a snack & wait for all the guests to arrive!
When you're ready, the Treasure Hunt can begin!

•

The backdoor, off the kitchen, had one more balloon in each color – but each had a child's name written on it. Attached to each balloon was a strand of yarn. The parents asked Matt where Carol was – Matt didn't know, but he covered, suggesting that she was part of the Treasure Hunt, or maybe inside still, working on some party game. Maybe Carol had explained this to him last night when he should have been listening. Knowing Carol, this was all part of the plan: some elaborate ritual, some carefully-planned surprise, some over-the-top reveal for her birthday boy.

Cade was their only child, and he could have been a carbon-copy of Carol. He was a little slight, although not as thin as his mother. Already he showed aptitude in music and art. Matt would try to play rough and tumble games with him, throw the ball, get him to watch a game, or go along with him to a job site once in a while, but he was always happiest with his mother. When she would carve out a long afternoon for practicing, he would lean up against the base of the small grand piano that had been a wedding present – that they really didn't have space for – and just seem to absorb the music. Sometimes he'd draw along with his mother's playing, or quietly read a book, but mostly he just seemed to be listening with his whole body. When Matt would catch a glimpse of this, usually when he happened to walk by the spare bedroom, he'd feel an urge to shut the door — as if he was witnessing something intimate, something he shouldn't see.

They'd turned that spare room into a music room early on, before they'd even known Cade would come to be. When they'd first married, and moved to this split-level ranch, he'd helped sell it to Carol by promising there'd be room for the piano. He'd thought maybe the living room — a long open space more like a landing, but she'd pursed her lips and shook her head, insisting she'd want privacy and quiet. She couldn't possibly share that space with a TV, she said, the space between her eyebrows frowning in irritation even as she tried to keep her mouth neutral. So he'd ripped out the carpeting in the spare room, taken out the paneling, redone it into a "perfect white cube" (that's what she said she wanted), and installed a few acoustic panels along the walls, hung symmetrically. She said she loved the high transom windows and the way they let in the light. It did make it easier when she began taking in students — that room, with the door.

Once the children discovered the balloons with their names on them, and figured out how the Treasure Hunt worked, it was impossible to get them to wait. Once the last child arrived, they were off. Matt opened the back and front door of the house, and the sunlight and fresh air permeated each room. He invited parents in, and they laughed at their children carefully following their assigned piece of yarn, high and low, up and over furniture, stepping over and through each other, focused totally on the trail they were following.

The parents were amazed. Carol's plan was a wonder. While Matt was sleeping, the house was transformed.

She'd put away each and every knickknack and breakable thing, so the children could crawl over everything to follow their treasure, their own individual map.

She'd closed the door to the music room, the bedrooms, the bathroom, but everywhere else in the house was fair game, and the spiderweb of yarn traversed the house high and low. The children shrieked and screamed, flushed with exertion.

She'd anticipated confusion, so every once in a while, the child's particular trail was tagged with their name, just to ensure they were still on track. Any potential argument quickly diffused.

She'd anticipated worries about what to do with the accumulated yarn, once followed. Each child was given a cardboard tube for winding. At strategic points, a new tube, tagged with the child's name, was tied onto the yarn treasure trail.

But mostly, she'd anticipated that even pleasure can flag. It was around seven months into their marriage, lying in bed with Matt, that Carol had begun to wonder if even this could last, if even this would be enough. She loved him, of course, and he loved her. He said it, and showed her every chance he got. They were past the honeymoon, and the settling into the house, and lying there, both of their breathing returning to normal, he was tracing the shapes of her areola and nipple with the callused pad of his fingertips. When he did this a few minutes earlier, it had brought her quickly into that final circle of pleasure, the place where she knew she would beat out her own intimate rhythm onto his body. It was a joke between them: his working man hands, her ultra-sensitive nipples. A touch there was often a question, an answer. She laid there, him lightly touching her, and wondered if this pleasure would be enough to sustain her.

The week before, she'd gone to the local high school to see if the choir needed an accompanist. They didn't. She'd talked with the choir director, the music teacher, the band director, about work. She'd played for them – she played beautifully. They'd never heard anyone play so beautifully. She was a wonder, she was classically trained, she had a master's in music performance. And here she was in this small town, with her little baby grand, all this time on her hands, a man who loves her, and afraid already of the unhappiness arriving soon. But then Matt remodeled the music room so she could take on students. And then she had Cade.

·

Knowing that the difficulty of untangling crisscrossing yarn could begin to weigh on eight-year-olds, that the initial flush of pleasure could begin to wear off, Carol planted small treasures along the way for each of them. Somehow, in the way of mothers, she knew what each of them most desired.

The girl with the purple balloon loved purple, all things purple – she always had. At one point, her yarn became bright purple, flecked with silver, and led her into the kitchen where it wrapped three times around the refrigerator door and slipped inside. Inside was a can of grape soda. Soda (soda wasn't allowed at the girl's house) and grape (so sweet to be cloying, so purple it would stain the teeth). Because at this point all the other treasure-hunters were diverted to the basement, the girl took a quick look around and glugged the sweet sticky nearly in one swallow. Soon her belly would ache, but no one would know why – all they'd had outside where healthy snacks (and how the parents had smirked when they'd seen that . . . *you know Carol,* they'd said, *she's never understood children,* they'd said). And what even the girl didn't know is that Carol had been in the kitchen watching.

Another boy, who had three older brothers and two older sisters, and never had anything for himself, followed his treasure-trail down to the basement and found a room with a lock on the inside, and inside was *Mousetrap* and *Operation* and other games with lots of small little parts. All those games that a younger sibling never gets to play, because by the time they're handed down all the parts are missing anyway, and the boy locked the door from the inside and played and played, listening with pleasure to each startling buzz as he worked and worked at the wishbone and the funny bone and the rubber band that connects the ankle bone to the knee bone, until the furious knocking on the door forced him out. Carol saw that too.

For one boy, who she'd run into with his mother school shopping with Cade, who'd stood fascinated by the row of different colored pens and markers at the point-of-sale display, trying each on the piece of scrap paper, until his mother yelled at him, grabbed him roughly by the shoulder. The mother had told him to "stop scribbling," and "you don't need all those colors!" Carol and Cade had both ducked their heads, but the mother had seen them. So Carol bought all twenty-one colors for the boy, tied them in intervals along his yarn. With each new color, a little more of this memory came back to the mother, and she felt shamed, felt judged. She looked around for Carol and was glad she couldn't see her.

Each of the children's desires grew greater as they continued along the Treasure Hunt. Carol knew that happiness is desire with the certainty of fulfillment.

As Carol was setting up the Treasure Hunt the night before, unwinding the rainbow of color, hooking yarn across furniture, behind curtain rods, around spindles, and between table legs, she could feel it spooling out of her. When Cade was born something had gone wrong; they hadn't cut the cord right, and ever since then, wherever he went in the world, however far he went away from her, she felt an ever-tug between his body and hers. Her interior was like a halved spaghetti squash, all strings, and she was scraped and spooned out by the day-to-day until she was only a flimsy shell. The light shone through; she couldn't hold form.

Wherever she was, she had a need to touch things. If her fingers weren't laying on the cool ivory of the piano keys, she pantomimed playing the most difficult pieces: Rachmaninov, or Beethoven's Hammerklavier. Matt told her she tapped his body in her sleep. She took to counting her bites, following an internal metronome in her head. She tried to slow down the tempo each day, moving from adagietto to adagio, from adagio to largo. She dreamed of lentissimo. During the day, she imagined every room Cade inhabited, counting the steps he must take from the art room to his classroom, from the classroom to the bathroom. She volunteered at the school so she could have a mental blueprint in her head, to allow her to better imagine his days, the shape of his hours. Matt said their sex had become "mechanical." He said she was getting "too thin." At dinner, he watched her move the food around her plate, eagle-eyed. She bought him hand lotion, balms, said the feel of his hands – the catch and hook of his weathered skin – bothered her.

●

For the girl with the purple balloon, the end of the Treasure Hunt led her into the back basement. She had been in a room like this before but hadn't been able to get out. Her uncle had blocked the door, and she had frozen. On the table was a tangle of hammers. The girl thought she heard someone whisper *smash the windows* . . . so she did. She took the hammers to the high basement windows, where a ladder had been positioned in front of each. After tapping timidly at each pane of glass, she broke through, ringed around the frame and knocked loose each stray shard. She shimmied out easily, and this time the blood bore witness to her escape.

The boy with the many many colors of pens was led to the upstairs hallway, where a fire escape ladder was hung out the window. He'd seen the same ladder under the bed in his parents' room, dreamed of the day he'd be a hero, leading them all to safety. He put on the child-sized fireman's hat that waited on the floor for him, shimmied down the ladder, and jumped to the ground, to the new-spring green grass outside. If he would color it he'd use his fine-tipped art pens, mixing *lime* with *clover*.

The boy with the yellow balloon's yarn-trail led to the door to the music room. On the door was a note with his name on it: only he could go into that room. Inside, there were dolls – all the dolls his sisters had, that he wasn't allowed to play with. Boys didn't play with dolls. Boys didn't pick out outfits, or brush hair, or pick out colors for their toes. Boys didn't sit by themselves and play. He closed the door and in the quiet of the room, the clean white space of the room, he dressed them and brushed their hair, and told them how pretty they were. They told him how pretty he was too.

•

The parents left, all angry. They wanted to talk to Carol, but no one could find Carol. Matt apologized and apologized. The children each had a bundle of gifts: they'd be carefully picked over, and some discarded. Each had a secret smile, each knew they'd been seen. Carol had disappeared – but Matt and Cade knew she was there. Over the coming days and months and years, they would hear her playing the piano, feel her slight weight on the couch, or in the bed next to them. They'd hear her voice, a whisper-sibilance, but didn't know how to explain to anyone else why they couldn't see her. If anyone had asked, they'd say the last time she'd been visible was before Cade's eighth birthday party, before she'd finished the Treasure Hunt, before that final unspooling.

Cade grew up, continuing to look more and more like his mother: brown-ginger hair, scattered freckles across his nose and cheeks. He'd have children of his own, and they too looked like their grandmother. Every once in a while, someone would ask after her: *How's your mother? Is she still . . .?* and trail off. No one knew how to address Carol's state – her not-being. Her invisibility. *She's still around,* Cade would say, *still the same.* Carol enjoyed her grandchildren. Matt never remarried or dated. There was nobody to serve papers to, there was no body. In pictures of the extended family, there's an empty space that may or may not be Carol, a space that may or may not be blank, a whisper-space of an invisible woman, who began disappearing long ago, and finished disappearing the day her boy turned eight, when she translated her corporeality into the dreams and desires of children and let them each see that there are rooms where they could be themselves, where they could lock the door, where they could escape, if they needed to.

Hand-Me-Down

They were sitting at the decrepit picnic table on the back lawn, between the cracked tennis courts no one played on anymore, and the basement patio. The late summer grass had grown long, bent over and soft. He stretched out his long legs toward the field just beyond the property line. She watched the dark hair on his calves move a little in the breeze. She'd taken off her shoes to rest her feet in the grass, and in between its softness, could feel hard bits of acorns, some sharp pine needles. He was telling her why Tiana had left. Why he'd decided to stay. How his childhood home had begun to feel like home again, but Tiana had said she wouldn't stay in that house, in that town.

The house – four bedrooms, formal sitting rooms, three bathrooms – loomed behind them, stretching its two stories from the foundation built into the hill to high roof peak. It sat back from the ring of a large cul-de-sac. About a year and a half ago, when his mother was terminal, Sean had come back home. His father had begged him for help caring for her, and reluctantly, he agreed. His brother only came for short visits – one at the beginning; one at the end. They'd turned one of the ground-level sitting rooms into her bedroom: a hospital bed with rails, wheeled tables, a big screen TV, her knitting projects. Anything to keep her as

173

comfortable and occupied as possible. Despite the doctors' best estimates, she'd lived for sixteen more months. There were as many or as few chairs as necessary for friends who came to visit. A lot in the beginning, only a few in the end.

Carly Jo hadn't known Sean was home until she'd run into him at the local gas station. Upon recognizing his profile, she thought she was seeing a ghost. She'd last seen him at graduation – or a party that weekend – before he'd left town, left her, and their small group of friends, swearing he was never coming back to "this fucking backward town." As far as she'd known, he never had. Holiday weekends when she'd run into people from high school back visiting, congregating back at the one bar open on Christmas Eve and Day, people would ask: *What ever happened to Sean? Are you still in touch?* She'd try to imitate her best wry smile, hiding that his leaving town meant leaving her, too; hiding that even his parents seemed happy about their severing. When they crossed paths, his parents pretended not to know her. She was the girl they'd never liked; the one his mother had once warned him *not to get into trouble.*

When Carly Jo had heard through the town's grapevine about his mother's first diagnosis, she hadn't known how to feel. Sadness for Sean, sure. But she knew that if she'd seen his mother out, she wouldn't be able to say anything. All those years and the scabs were still on, thick with a vein of blood just below the surface. Her parents brought home a church bulletin that announced: "Prayers requested for Mrs. Mary Hodgekiss, on hospice care," and she'd gathered it was back.

•

A week later, she would see Sean at the Kwik Trip, his arms loaded with chips, a six-pack, and a bag of milk. He was looking at the small pharmacy offerings. She was just about to say hello, to say she was sorry to hear about his mom, when he'd turned and brightened. He set down everything he was holding and hugged her. One good thing about those bags of milk is that they have strong seams.

Carly Jo was caught off guard, and then a woman walked up, gingerly holding a bottle of wine. "Um, Sean? I guess I'll get this . . ." Both women stopped and looked at each other across the tall frame of the man between them.

"Tiana, this is my best friend from high school," and the woman came forward and hugged her. With her face in Tiana's fragrant hair, she could hear Sean continuing the conversation, repeating her name – Carly Jo, Carly Jo. She'd been trying to work on her reciprocation of physical affection lately, to respond to others' cues, so she held Tiana's thin shoulders for a three-second count. A respectable length of a hug (it seemed to her) for this perfect stranger, who was with this now-stranger she used to love.

•

Over those months, they saw each other often and Carly Jo swallowed everything she was feeling. Sean said he needed her, he missed her; he wanted to get out of the house, away from his mom and her dying and the hospice aids and nurses and the visitors who didn't know what to say but kept looking to him for some kind of help. Sean said his dad shambled around the house from room to room, going up and down the stairs, moving this item or that, then putting it back. Sean said Tiana visited a couple weekends a month and they should all hang out; they'd really get along. Sean said sometimes he wished his mother would hurry up with her dying, that it was all taking so long. Sean said he couldn't believe he said that; he didn't mean it, he just didn't know who to talk to. Sean said his job was flexible and he was able to telecommute, so he would stay as long as he was needed.

Carly Jo was as surprised as Tiana when, after his mom did die, he decided to stay. His dad worked out some deal between Sean and his brother and gave Sean the house as part of an early inheritance. After the funeral, his dad left to live in a condo someplace warm – that was all she could remember of the details of him leaving. He packed some clothes and a toiletry kit, shut the door to the bedroom in the house he'd shared with his wife, and got in his car. Carly Jo was pulling into the double driveway as he backed out, and he'd lightly hit his horn as he passed her. She watched Sean and Tiana, holding hands like any couple, waving in front of the garage's open doors, the inside stuffed with a family's worth of junk, the asphalt cracked and sprouting weeds.

Over the next few weeks, she'd get a text from time to time – most of them were from Tiana. Tiana would send pictures of herself and Sean, with some dusty art project unearthed from the crawlspace or basement. Sean's parents saved everything: every report card and event program and kid's drawing and article of clothing in a box or pile somewhere in that house. There was the photo of Sean trying to fit into his middle-school gym shorts – greyed once-black fabric piped in yellow stretched over his muscular thigh – his face split by a wide grin. There were the snaps of the yearbook photos accompanied by Tiana's numerous emojis: young Sean and young Carly Jo at the senior prom, at homecoming; in the school newspaper, in the school play. There was a shot of under the sink in the ground floor bathroom, adjacent to what had been his mother's dying-room: row after row of pills. Tiana sent this particular picture with no caption or emojis and no Sean. There was a series of each of them wearing a short blonde wig, hamming it up. Carly Jo recognized it right away: it was the wig Sean's mom had worn after she lost her hair.

Two weeks later, Tiana was gone. Carly Jo never really thought she would stay. From the first time she'd met her, looking for a bottle of wine at the gas station, hair smoothed and styled, her expensive scent transferred in that hug, she'd wondered how she'd make it there. She'd deleted the photos Tiana'd sent but kept thinking of her face framed by Sean's mom's cancer hair. Wigs like that, made with real hair, cost a lot of money. She deleted Tiana's contact info from her phone.

•

The first time she and Sean slept together she was fifteen – so was he. They'd been in the basement of someone's house, at a cast party for the musical. She'd had a bit part, maybe one line. Sean was in the chorus and did some basic dancing. They'd spent most of the rehearsal time sitting cross-legged back stage and letting the long black curtains pool around them, creating caverns of moted light. At the dress rehearsal, Carly Jo had grabbed a bag of lemon wedges from the dressing room and they'd each taken turns eating them – the English teacher director had said something about lemons being good for clearing their throats. But they'd sucked the pulp of each bitter piece, letting the juice tighten and toughen their mouths until they ended up sweaty and kissing beneath the weight of the dusty stage curtains, missing their cues.

They got it together for the performance, but as soon as they got to the after party they found a quiet place in the basement and devoured each other, not knowing or caring who might walk down and see them. After, as Carly Jo was pulling her t-shirt back on over her head, her back cold and gritty from the silver-flecked floor, Sean had flipped on the light. A counter ran all alongside the back wall. They started pulling out drawers and bins by their little wooden handles, and found a small porcelain sink, a series of tubes, a collection of little instruments. Back upstairs Carly Jo asked about the room, and the party's host said something about the house's original occupant being a dentist, practicing out of the basement office.

The second first time she and Sean slept together, after he came back home, he'd asked her if she remembered the basement dentist office. Sean had been removing her shirt just then, asking about 'tools,' and laughter burbled out of her. His face was resting between her breasts, just his nose and forehead showing.

"I always think of it when I'm at the dentist's," Carly Jo gasped, lifting her hips up off the couch to slide her jeans down. Sean's face continued its movement down, to her belly, further, kissing the beginning of her hair, moving his hands around under her, hooking his thumbs under the fabric of her underwear. Carly Jo inhaled sharply and lifted herself again, pushing up and against his face, feeling his breath warm her. He said something, and the words disappeared into her. She felt the whisper of his lips move on her lips.

"What?"

He said it again. She moved away from him slightly, her whole body a river, aching for him, wanting him with everything she'd been trying to keep him from knowing since she'd first seen him in that gas station months before.

"No, Sean, what did you say?"

He looked up at her, his hazel eyes darkened, liquid. "Guess what this room was?"

As he said this, her body moved toward him again, remembering the way those "s's" and "m's" had pressed into her, hummed and buzzed her alive.

"What?" she asked.

"A funeral parlor . . ."

Her body stilled. What he said made sense but she'd never thought of it before: the two front rooms separated by a large central door. Both formal and identical. The rest of the house set apart and separated by another wooden door. They hadn't spent much time at his house when his mother was alive. She wondered if this was the room where they laid bodies in state, where they held services.

Her body was no longer humming. She'd gone cold. Sean kept moving, his mouth over her body, removing her clothes, and she went along with it. She let him.

In October, Carly Jo pulled up to the house and pressed the garage remote, Sean having recently cleared a space for her car. A hard frost had been predicted for that night, and she didn't want to scrape the windshield in the morning before her shift. A rabbit sat in the middle of the open space, frozen and staring at her. She waited for it to move – it didn't. She put the car in park, and hoping to scare it out, opened the car door. The rabbit bolted, fitting itself into a pile of boxes. She didn't want to run it over when she pulled in, but she didn't know how to get it out. She slowly moved toward the boxes into the yellowed light cast by the overhead light. She turned off the car, and went in, leaving the door open.

"Sean?" she yelled into the kitchen. No answer. "Sean?"

On the walls alongside the stairs, hung photos of young Sean, his brother who stayed away for most of his mother's dying, several portraits of his parents, all matted in muted colors. When she yelled his name down into the basement, he called back. When he got up to the kitchen, she told him about the rabbit in the garage, how it must have been stuck in there all day. He grabbed a flashlight from the kitchen drawer and went out.

"Where?" he asked, sounding exasperated as he surveyed the garage. She pointed to the narrow space between stacked boxes where it disappeared.

"Here?" He kicked the boxes.

"Don't scare it." She got down on her knees, looking for evidence of fur, to see where it went. They started unloading the pile from the top down – a tricycle, some plastic toys – when the rabbit shot out and ran under his car. Carly Jo went around the other side and found the rabbit by the car's back wheel. She heard the other garage door open, saw Sean's shoes on the other side of the car. "It's back here," she said.

The flashlight's beam swept under the car, catching and holding the trembling rabbit. Carly Jo watched until it rushed past her, darting for another pile of boxes. Sean had retrieved a broom from somewhere. "Why don't we just leave the door open and let it run out?" she asked.

"You're not helping," Sean said, smacking the junk pile with the broom handle.

Carly Jo went inside the house.

About twenty minutes later, he came inside. She didn't ask what happened.

•

She couldn't sleep. Sean had taken to sleeping in his parents' old room, but he hadn't moved or changed anything. There were still framed pictures of them on the nightstands by both sides of the bed. The baskets of dried flowers that his mother used to decorate all over the house were still arranged on the top of the dresser and armoire, collecting dust. The matching sheets and dust ruffles – decorated with small chintz flowers – were his mother's taste. She couldn't bring herself to ask how often he did the laundry. When he'd start kissing her, moving his hand down between her legs, she'd close her eyes and try to pretend they were somewhere else – some other room they were colonizing. It was better when he'd come to her apartment, when she could

181

be in a space that didn't remind her of his mother, of her body and her dying. She'd make up excuses to get him to come to her place, but she couldn't do that all the time, so sometimes she just went along with it, trying to imagine the old Sean, the old Carly Jo, who they were.

When she suggested cleaning out the house – offering to take things to the second-hand store, to handle his mother's clothing for him – he'd snapped at her. He said that when his father came back to visit he'd want things to look the same. He said that he didn't feel right letting her touch his mother's things. He said those were the things from his childhood and he'd decide what happened to them.

The space he'd cleared in the garage for her car ended up filling back in. The rabbit had been there a few more times, stock still in the middle of the small open space, staring at her when she opened the door by remote. She worried more and more about accidentally killing it, making a pile of guts and fur in the middle of garage. She knew it was just a fucking rabbit, but it shouldn't have been there, it didn't make any sense. She felt like it was mocking her. If she told Sean, he'd end up being an asshole. She felt sorry for the rabbit, for its fear. Between all the shit in the garage and the rabbit, she felt like she was being forced away. She never told Sean about seeing it again.

•

The night she realized what he was doing is what ended them. They were at her apartment. She'd been just about to come: his mouth between her legs, his tongue flicking back and forth; her thigh muscles tensing as she pushed herself harder and harder against his mouth, his fingers slippery with her, moving around and around her nipples, the side swells of her breasts. He paused, and covered the same area a second time, with intention.

She came back into herself. He was checking her — checking her breasts. She was in his mouth and moaning and he was checking her fucking breasts as some kind of fucked-up exam in some kind of fucked-up sexual routine.

She moved in one motion away from him, paddling her feet and knees like a runner backing away.

He said, "I thought . . . I thought I felt something." He reached his hand up to her side, to feel the skin under her arm, where her ribcage met the side of her breast.

"Don't," she said, hitting his hand away, her body shaking.

They were at her apartment with no pictures on the side tables but, in her mind, she could see Tiana wearing his mother's cancer wig — the blond bob changing her coloring, immortalizing her as once both familiar and strange. After Sean left, she turned the shower to the water's hottest setting and used lots of soap to scrub whatever traces of his hands from her body. Her eyes were closed, the water streaming down, and she felt it, under her right breast.

Her eyes opened, soap-filled. She took a deep breath and moved her left hand slowly along her side, then doubled back, ensuring that it wasn't just rib. There it was: a jellied spot under the skin. Carly Jo slowed her breathing and stretched right arm up and over her head. She started moving two finger pads in slow concentric circles.

Boundaries

They hadn't seen each other in twenty-five years and were avoiding the official reunion. Too many scheduled events, too much togetherness, too many people they weren't sure they really wanted to see again. When Sarah's former college roommate had originally floated the idea, she'd been unsure, but after a few months of texts and DMs, they'd agreed to meet mid-June, and just as a small group. Sarah and her husband, Kevin; former roommate and once-good friend Tully and her girlfriend, Gen; Tully's college girlfriend Monica and her husband David. When Sarah had mentioned the burgeoning plan to Kevin, he was uncertain, but game. He'd never met any of them but had heard plenty about Tully. When it came up at Easter dinner, her brother had laughed and told him not to go. "Those girls will eat you alive," he warned Kevin. Sarah flung a forkful of mashed potatoes at him.

Monica and David found the rental through an online search. It was available when they wanted, there were no neighboring rentals, and it was on a small lake. The pictures showed an old wooden pier, and the grey rocks of the Adirondacks stacked higher and higher, lichen-covered and casting shade, ringed the lake. That's probably why it was so undeveloped, yet stunningly beautiful, just inside the blue line that marked the original borders of the park. The driveway was a long, rutted gravel and dirt lane with a humped track of grass in the middle, only accessible in the summer. Enough bedrooms, acres of woods. Poor cell reception, but WIFI. Bring food and linens. Split three ways it wasn't too expensive.

Sarah and Kevin planned to arrive that Friday and spend a long weekend, then see if they wanted to stay the week. They could change their return tickets – they'd both taken the week off from work. Tully and Gen, and Monica and David, were planning on staying the whole week.

Sarah had tried to explain to Kevin that even though Tully and Monica had been together all of college, they split up soon after; how even though she'd always thought Monica was only into girls, she guessed she'd been wrong; how somehow, even after all these years, Tully and Monica were still close – still family, and no, David didn't seem to mind. Kevin said that was enough reason for the visit – to see how that whole dynamic worked.

•

In the kitchen, Tully and Monica were putting away groceries, searching in cupboards for pots and pans, a decent knife or two, hand-washing glasses and plates in advance of their use. Sarah walked in, through the pollen-matted screen door, and it closed with a muffled flap. The scene before her took her back to college. Monica was holding up glasses to the light, scraping rims and looking again, shaking her head and plunging the drinking vessels into soapy water, complaining that the water wasn't hot enough. Tully was making jokes about her germ phobias, hands on her ex-girlfriend's hips, her chin resting on her shoulder, whispering in her ear. They looked like they were still in love, still together. Sarah paused, Kevin crashing into her from behind.

David was perched on a barstool, laughing at the two women at the sink, and when he heard the noise from the door, he jumped up to grab Sarah's bag out of her hand.

"Hi," he smiled widely, his beard dark and contrasting sharply with his teeth. "You must be Sarah." The women at the sink turned and yelled – squealed really – and Sarah rushed past David, hugging the two together, then Tully, then Monica. Monica's hands were wet and covered with bubbles of dish soap, the foam sliding down her forearms. Tully grabbed Sarah again, holding her longer, and the two women swayed: bodies pressed together, chest and belly and legs, chins fitting into each other's soft shoulders. It had been more than two decades since they'd seen each other and each thought the other looked exactly the same; they were both wrong and right.

Monica stood next to them, her right hand softly on Tully's back as she felt her dear friend and former love laugh and cry, her body wracked with the emotional strain of it all. Over by the door, the two men stood side-by-side, quiet, not yet greeting each other or doing anything else to interrupt the moment. Sunlight streamed in the window over the sink, and the counter was a messy array of bakery goods and fruit and a few skillets, two cartons of brown eggs, and another grocery bag, yet unpacked. The beer and liquor and mixers were all still in the back of David and

Monica's car. The men would get to that first and have a chance to talk, away from the women and away from the house.

Sarah broke the embrace, "Where's Gen?"

"She's checking out *the grounds*," Monica answered.

"There's supposed to be a shed with canoes or kayaks or something," Tully explained. David cleared his throat, still standing by the door, holding tight to the handles of Sarah's suitcase. "Oh, David!" Tully rushed in, moving toward the men. "And you must be Kevin," she extended her arms, hugging Sarah's husband, holding him a beat or two longer than is usual with strangers, "I'm Tully, so nice," and here she turned back to Sarah, winking, "to *finally* meet you."

"You too," Kevin said, squirming a little, as Tully hadn't fully let go of his torso.

"This is David, Monica's husband," and through some awkward maneuvering the men set down what they were holding and shook hands, "and that's Monica." Monica had dried her hands and came over to hug Kevin too. Over her shoulder, Kevin caught his wife's eye and she shrugged. This was more hugging than Kevin was used too – he wasn't a hugger and he didn't think Sarah was either, but clearly hugging was going to be a big part of the weekend. David picked up Sarah's bag, and Monica took Kevin's from where he'd set it down.

"I'll show you your room," Monica said, and began leading the group out of the kitchen, and through a dining room and a living room with mismatched furniture, to stairs against the back wall. "We gave you the honeymoon suite," she said, as she clomped heavily up the stairs, her well-shaped, tan calves moving in and out of Kevin's eyeline. There was no railing on the stairs. Behind Kevin, David followed, and somewhere behind him was his wife, Sarah. He heard her laugh from the bottom of the stairs.

•

After unloading the cars, unpacking, finally getting the kitchen to Monica's specifications, and Gen rejoining the group, they opened beers or made drinks in plastic cups and drifted out to the dock. The wood was greyed with age, but dried to a silvered cast, and hewn with what looked like tree trunks and four-by-fours. Sturdy, no visible nails. After a quick once-over, Monica pronounced the dock safe. They spent the afternoon jumping into and lazily swimming in the cool mountain water, the bottom clearly visible, with not even a minnow or frog or turtle showing itself. After more than a few, they had an echo contest, their voices bouncing off the rock walls and answering them back. Even after the sun began to disappear behind the trees, there were no bugs whining or biting.

Gen pronounced it "perfect solitude," her hand resting proprietarily on Tully's upper thigh. David and Kevin went to start the salmon, and Sarah noticed the beginning throb of a migraine in her left temple. Too much sun and fresh air after the early morning waking and flight, then another couple hours from the airport. She took a Relpax, and drank two big glasses of water. Kevin was sitting on a stump by the grill, next to a pile of empties when she headed in to the house, and she stopped to kiss his cheek. He seemed to be having fun. David was in the middle of a story, using the long-handled grill tongs to gesticulate, and Kevin's laugh pitched higher, the way it did when he was well into his cups. She told him she had a little headache and was just going to lie down before dinner. He promised to check on her, and wake her when it was time to eat.

Some time later, the bed shook a little and she opened her eyes to Monica staring down at her. Long lashes, the kind of blue that looks crystalline, the way early frost makes patterns on window panes and bare branches on really cold mornings before the snow falls. Her headache was still there, but had expanded to the right side, leaving a lingering band around the back of her skull. "Feeling better?"

"Not really," Sarah answered, "Just a little too much today, maybe." If they hadn't taken an early flight from Lincoln, the whole day would have been wasted. And she'd probably only gotten five hours of sleep the night before.

"What do you take? I get migraines too."

"Something every day, I can't remember the name. And then a rescue pill, Relpax."

"Oh, I've got Imitrex." Monica had laid down next to her and was softly smoothing her hair back from her forehead, fluttering her fingers on the soft spot at the sides of her head where she most wanted pressure.

"I tried that, but it didn't work for me."

"We've got weed."

"Thanks, maybe. Food might help too." Monica pressed two fingers right into her temples, momentarily redirecting the pain. Sarah closed her eyes. She wasn't sure how long she laid there with Monica's fingers in exactly the right spot, holding the beast in her head at bay. She opened them when she sensed someone else in the room.

"Everything OK?" It was Kevin. Sarah sat up, quickly, jostling Monica.

"Yup, just coming down."

•

Dinner was delicious: center-cut salmon in a butter, parsley, and dill sauce, layered with sliced lemon and oranges and red onion; a spring mix salad; fresh bread from the bakery in town; wine and more wine. Foreheads and noses were pink from the afternoon in the water and everyone's eyes were crinkling tired. Sarah drank only water, still trying to hydrate away her headache. Every once in a while, she'd catch Monica looking at her, sympathetic. Kevin chewed rhythmically.

"You're humming," she said to him, as he was digging into his second piece of fish.

"Do you hear it?"

She laughed, "Yes, that's why I mentioned it."

"Not me – the sound."

Gen's eyes met his across the table. "I can feel it," she said.

"It sounds like a generator is running somewhere," he answered her.

"What?" David wanted to know.

"There's a sound," Kevin answered. They all quieted their chewing and listened.

"I don't hear anything," Tully offered.

"Me neither," said David.

191

"I know what you mean," that was Gen. "I've felt it all day." Tully covered Gen's hand with her own.

"Gen's really in tune with her body – always feeling things I don't. It's because of the body work she does." Gen's hand stayed still under Tully's. She looked at Kevin again, held his eyes, no blink.

"You can feel it too?" she asked him.

"I can hear it. I didn't realize I was humming."

"Maybe that's what's causing your headache," Monica turned to Sarah.

"No," Sarah reached for her water again. She'd taken another rescue pill. Sometimes eating something and then sleeping helped. "It's just the long day of travel – we got up so early this morning and flying always dehydrates me." She nodded at her husband. "I should have remembered to drink more water throughout the day." Her left eye drooped a little, and she winced whenever anyone set down forks or knives directly on their plates. She inclined her head toward her husband, remembering how quickly she accepted the drink he poured for her on the dock, then the second, then another two that David made extra strong (she thought). She should have had a snack; she should have had a water for every drink. She shouldn't have been so quick to forget she was forty-seven years old, even though when she looked around seeing Tully and Monica made it easy to pretend they were back somewhere in their shared past. If she'd looked a little harder, she would have seen Gen, and David, and Kevin – her Kevin, and known what year it was. She could have looked at her arms and noticed how the skin hung loose when she moved, or how her ankles seemed thick, or down at her stomach and seen evidence of her daughters and known what year it was. She couldn't day drink and not pay the consequences. Two pills and still no relief was a bad migraine; she hoped it wouldn't continue into tomorrow, ruining the weekend. She wanted to change the subject. "What kind of body work do you do Gen?"

Tully answered for her, "What doesn't she do?" Her hand was still covering Gen's, trying to hold it.

"I work at a studio, yoga and Pilates classes, but also take on private clients," Gen's index finger started moving slightly, caressing the underside of her girlfriend's cupped palm.

"That's how we met," Tully beamed.

"Well, I'm how you met," David interrupted, smiling.

"Oh right, David! If it weren't for David, or Cupid as we call him, we never would have met . . ." Tully launched into the story, with occasional interjections by David or Monica, of how she'd started attending yoga classes taught by Gen, working up her courage to talk to her at the juice bar after, and finally asking her out. But it was all David's doing really. David who told Tully about Gen in the first place, the new-to-Northampton yoga teacher he thought she'd like. David first scoped out whether Gen was single, whether she was queer, and then arranged for Monica to come to a few classes first to determine whether Gen was good enough for Tully.

"Really," and David turned to Kevin for this comment, "I just wanted to make sure Tully was off the market for good, so I wouldn't have to worry," and he winked at Sarah. Kevin stiffened a little in his chair, but Sarah didn't think anyone else caught it. He continued, "You know how it is Kevin, being with a bi woman – never being quite sure if you're really enough for her."

At that, Monica elbowed her husband, knocking the wine in her glass all over what little remained on her plate. A deep red Syrah drowned the small bits of lettuce in the deep-rimmed plate. David jumped up to avoid any splatter, and Kevin did too. Kevin continued to the kitchen for the paper towels, returning with the whole roll, far more than was needed for the small accident. Beneath the table was a braided rug, the kind made with cast-off rags rolled and stitched together. It absorbed the wine quickly, the new red-brown stain indistinguishable from the existing pattern.

When Monica extracted the vape from her purse and began passing it around, both Sarah and Kevin demurred. Sarah hadn't smoked in a long time and wasn't sure how it would affect her head, and Kevin didn't smoke. They offered to clean up. While they were side-by-side at the sinks, washing and drying dishes, they were mostly quiet. The others had moved onto the couch in the living room.

"Bad?"

"One of the worst I've had," Sarah answered. Even the dim yellowed light over the sink made her squint.

"I can finish up here."

"We're almost done; then I'll go to bed."

Kevin sighed audibly, took the handful of mismatched silverware she offered. "What did David mean by that?" He paused, "By 'being with a bi woman'?"

Sarah added the last stack of plates to the cooling water. "You know."

194

"Well, I know you dated women in the past, but, it's not like you're 'bi'."

From behind them, they heard a noise and turned to see Monica standing, her phone in hand. "Um, sorry, you guys, I was just wondering if either of you were able to get the wifi to work?"

"No, we couldn't figure it out either," Sarah answered.

"OK, oh well. Guess not everything can be as perfect as advertised." She sort of skipped back to the living room, her shoulder-length curly hair bouncing with her, and the bottom of her feet patterning a rhythm on the dark lino-leum. Monica had pronounced the house perfect earlier, not even a hint of mildew or mold smell. Sarah heard Kevin humming.

"You're humming again."

"You really don't hear that?"

"No."

"What I mean is – do you still think of yourself as bi?" He swallowed the last of the wine in his glass, handed it to her to wash. "Are you still attracted to women?"

"Do you really want to talk about this now? Here?"

"No. We can go upstairs."

"When I get upstairs, I'm going to sleep," she pulled the plug in the bottom of the sink, watched the water level get lower and lower until the spiral began and picked up speed, gurgling and leaving a small pile of detritus in the strainer.

After wishing everyone good night, Sarah crawled under the covers without so much as washing her face or brushing her teeth. She'd managed to take off her shorts, but kept her panties on, and the undershirt she wore in lieu of a bra when she was feeling lazy and wanted to be comfortable, and her t-shirt. The throb in her head had moved to her jaw, shaking her fillings. She put a pillow over her face, drowning out all the light, praying the cool temperature of the fabric would provide a little relief. Even so, she heard Kevin ask if she'd ever been with Tully. She shook her head as slightly as she could without dislodging the small islands of pain that lived inside her skull. When Kevin sat down on his side of the bed, she felt a wave of nausea threaten; when he flapped the sheet and coverlet, trying to get comfortable, she gripped the mattress with both fists. The pain was a weight holding her in place, thick on her closed lids, her temples, the soft give of skin at the base of her throat. Her ears were stopped with a rushing of wings. She heard him ask "What about Monica?"

•

In the morning, Sarah woke to an empty space in the bed. She'd slept terribly. The migraine had kept up its cresting pain all night, and each time Kevin moved, or made noises – the incessant humming, talking in his sleep, even yelling a few times – she'd moaned and tried to retreat deeper down into the coil of sheets and blankets. She'd had a terrible nightmare: she dreamt she was walking, beneath a deep canopy of trees in the woods, where the air was stifling with heat, breezeless. Brush slapped her legs and arms, leaving a trail of bramble-scratch and nettled skin. She saw deer whose coats were horribly lumpy with ticks grown grotesque with feeding – waxy yellow and bundled on top of each other like bouquets. The only sound in the woods was a hum, low and barely discernible; no matter how long she walked she never came to a road.

Once she startled awake and thought she saw Monica's face, as if the woman had crouched down at her side of the bed, staring at her with concern. In the doorway, she made out another figure, one who looked like Gen. That was one of the times she heard Kevin yell – she thought she heard him say *Leave us alone*. But that would be so unlike him: to shout, to say something in anger at these near-strangers, these people who were her friends. That must have been part of the dream. She would have reached out for him, but she couldn't move; the pain pinioned her. She should have gotten up to drink more water, maybe take another pill, but she worried that moving would heighten the agony she was already in, that it was only beginning. Beneath the known pain was a continent of suffering. She didn't know how to get away from it, or stop it, so she stayed very still, too petrified to move.

After opening her eyes, she stayed immobile, not even moving her head. She could sense that Kevin wasn't in bed with her. He was good to let her sleep, but she missed him already. She listened to the sounds of people talking and laughing downstairs: she could smell coffee. Sometimes caffeine helped.

In the bathroom, she splashed water on her face, brushed her teeth, and her hair. Pulling the hairbrush through her short no-nonsense bob, she noticed her ear looked dark – she hooked the hair behind her ear and crouched as close as she could to the cloudy mirror. Dried blood, a deep rust – a strand of crust from the whorl to pitted hole in her

197

lobe, down the side of her neck to the crewneck of her t-shirt. She checked the bed and found a dried oblong on the mattress, another on the pillow, lacings of blood on the sheets and blankets she'd swam in throughout the night. She decided to shower.

When Sarah finally went downstairs, the four of them seemed surprised to see her. She was surprised not to see Kevin. Gen thought he and Sarah had left together – maybe gone into town. She said she'd heard their rental SUV early this morning, when she was doing her sunrise yoga on the dock. She thought maybe they'd gone searching for some cell service. Sarah tried to cover that she didn't know where Kevin was by saying he wanted to let her sleep, given how poorly she was feeling. Still, he could have left her a note. She wouldn't even have called last night a fight – it was just a tense discussion, maybe a little disagreement. They'd both been tired from all the traveling, and she wasn't feeling well, and in retrospect, she probably could have prepared him a little better for the weekend: for meeting her friends, which included someone she used to date ("But that was ages ago!" Monica would say), and that everyone would be more open and demonstrative than what he was used to. This would be the conversation they'd all have a little later, when it got nearer to noon, and Kevin still wasn't back. By then, Sarah would have been truly worried, and need someone to talk to, so she'd begin with Tully. What began with Tully would then include Monica, and Monica would then bring David in, and then Gen would end up part of the conversation too.

It would end with Gen offering to help Sarah, who was still miserable, by rubbing her legs and arms with a special salve she made of shea butter and cannabis oil, and doing some relaxation exercises in the darkened upstairs bedroom. Gen's voice was low and soothing, and her hands were the perfect mix of strong and gentle as they made long fluid movements up and down Sarah's limbs. She had Sarah lie on her back and close her eyes and she grasped her head, with a slight pulling motion, then let it rest in her hands, turning Sarah's head slightly side to side. Sarah felt like Gen's hands were a basket, and she was something precious. At the end, Gen still cradling her head, they just breathed together. It wasn't the sort of thing Sarah usually did – kind of hippie and touchy-feely, but she was willing to try anything. She was out of options and the migraine crouched in her left temple, flaring up whenever someone spoke with too many consonants stacked together or a little too loudly. Also, the room was dark. Apparently that salve had some effect – the stiffness she usually had in her left knee disappeared. Sarah did feel better for a little while after that – well enough to get a little angry at Kevin for up and leaving with no note and no notice. After lunch, they'd drive into town for some cell service so Sarah could call the girls and try to reach Kevin.

•

As soon as they found a main road, Sarah's phone lit up with two weak bars and started chiming with missed calls, texts, and two voicemails. None were from Kevin. Ali, their oldest had sent a picture of a pre-digital egg timer sitting atop a stove: the accompanying text said, "Grandma times our screen time." Another from Ali: "At Kaitlyn's. Josie at home bc she didn't do chores" and then some emojis. Sarah called Kevin's parents' house. His mother answered. After some pleasantries, and asking how the girls were, she asked to talk to Josie.

"Hi Mom," her youngest sounded unhappy. But she was twelve, so she often sounded this way.

"Hi Josie – how's your Saturday?"

"Grandma said I couldn't go anywhere because I didn't do my chores."

"What were you supposed to do?"

"Breakfast dishes and make my bed."

"And?"

"And I didn't make my bed."

"So?"

"So, I told her that I was going to take a nap later anyway and it didn't make sense to make it but she said that didn't matter because we make our beds in the morning."

"Josie, you're a guest which means –"

"When are you coming back?"

"Monday, probably."

"I hate it here," this was whispered, which probably meant her mother-in-law was hovering.

"Josie, be nice to Grandma and Pop Pop," Sarah heard her daughter's very audible sigh, despite the poor connection, and the wind past the half-opened window. "Have you talked to your father?"

"No, why? Isn't he with you?"

"Um, not right now – we don't have cell service at the house, and he went with another friend into town . . ." Sarah only felt bad for a minute lying to her daughter. She felt worse that he hadn't called them either.

"Did you have a fight?" Josie's nose for drama could always seem to sniff out if anything wasn't going right between her parents.

"No, Josie."

"Oh, did you get the text we sent of Grandma's timer?"

"Yup."

"You know, if I had my own phone, we could probably keep in touch better. Like, I could text you when Dad calls." Luckily Josie also had a short attention span.

"But I don't have cell service anyway, remember?"

"What kind of a place doesn't have cell service? Where are you?"

"It's beautiful," Sarah wasn't in the mood for this conversation, and they were pulling into town. Town meant a gas station with one pump next to a bakery and convenience store. There was a stop sign, but that was about it. They were in Tully and Gen's Rav-4, and Tully took the turn into the lot a little sharp, throwing Gen up against her closed window. "OK, I've got to go. Be nice to your grandparents and try to do what they ask of you."

"OK. Bye Mom."

"Bye Honey. I love you."

"Love you."

She hit 'end call' and looked up to see Tully watching her in the rear view. "Nothing?"

"He hasn't called them." Monica put her arm around her. She'd probably been touched more in the last twenty-four hours than she had been in the last month back home. Even David was looking at her across the back seat, sending sympathetic vibrations her way. Only Gen seemed apart, sitting straight-backed in the passenger seat, looking out the window.

"I don't feel it here," she said.

•

Kevin had been dead for almost nine hours.

He and his SUV had somehow lost the dirt-track driveway and ended up in the woods. His foot frantic on the accelerator, barely able to see, he'd gone an impressive way before he hit the tree – head on, at nearly 45 miles per hour. The pattern his head made when it hit the windshield, something like the pattern of ice freeze and refreeze on a winter's lake, could be imagined beautiful, if it weren't for the way it was also stained pink from the leaking head wound. Because he'd somehow gotten far enough away from the house, rushing to escape the hum, the flies had found him and were making quick work of the spilled fluids and broken skin. Blowflies work quickly to colonize flesh, laying their eggs – in a day or two they'd hatch. Blowfly maggots are called 'gentles.' Blowflies are the common name for these insects, so called because as the larvae hatch and grow, whatever-it-is seems to blow up many times its size, writhing as if alive again.

The house, and the land it sat on humming and throbbing, seemed to have a perimeter, and nothing living made

202

its home there. The woods were absent of any animal, or insect – even the water fishless. But beyond that boundary the natural world continued its work. Just then, as the group from the house was pulling into town, a deer walked up to the wrecked SUV with its open window and looking inside, sniffed the contents. Its nose may have nudged Kevin's arm a little, broken and wrenched through the steering wheel. The doe had an auburn coat, just russet, that would have been beautiful if it hadn't been crawling with ticks. It blinked its long-lashed eyes and moved on.

•

The bell above the door announced their entrance, and Sarah busied herself on her phone, calling and texting Kevin. The calls dropped. The texts went undelivered. She slow-walked to the front counter, where Tully was chatting up the girl at the register, asking questions about various breads and pastries, adding thoughtfully to the pile. She gushed about the bread they'd had last night, and for not the first time, Sarah wondered if she was high – if maybe she was most of the time. Now that she knew what a vape pen looked like, she'd noticed how often it was out or passed around. Whatever Gen had rubbed on her skin made her feel loose, less concerned than she probably should be about Kevin's disappearance and abdication of his parental duties. Now Tully was explaining that they were visiting, having an unorthodox twenty-fifth college reunion, although only three of them had been in college together. Sarah caught the young woman, whose nametag said Maria, looking at the group of five. Maybe she was trying to figure out who was whose, or who went to college together, or calculating their ages. She asked where they were staying and when Tully mentioned the turn-off right after the Route 8 sign, she straightened up.

"Those are bad woods," she said, quietly, no longer animated or making eye contact. At some point, Gen had come to stand next to Tully. At this pronouncement, Gen addressed the young woman.

"What do you mean?"

"You shouldn't be staying there," Maria rang up their purchases and put everything into a white paper bag.

"But it's beautiful – the lake and the woods, and there's no one around . . ." Tully started, but Gen put her hand on her forearm, squeezed a little.

"What do you mean?" she asked again, stepping forward into Maria's eyeline. But Maria didn't answer, she just closed the till and walked into the shadowed back of the store. On the drive home, Sarah noticed that Tully's forearm was bruising: four long finger marks and a short round one that must have been Gen's thumb.

•

Back on the dock and her head still throbbing, Sarah figured *Fuck it!* and finally accepted the vape pen, drawing too hard and sputtering, but reaching for it again and again. David came back in the canoe he'd taken to the center of the lake and announced he got a single bar out there. Sarah asked him to take her back out, and he did, and she left Kevin a long, angry voicemail.

Kevin – I cannot believe you just left me here this morning,

taking the car, without even so much as a note about
where you'd be. And now you've just, what? what?
shut off your cell? Blocked my calls? Are you really that
pissed? I'm so sorry that I didn't tell you that Monica
and I were together twenty-odd years ago, but who
cares? Tully doesn't care, and she dated Monica after
I did. David doesn't care and he's married to her!
At least I don't think he cares – David, do you care?
David's shaking his head, no, he does not care (we're in
a fucking canoe in the middle of the lake by the way,
because I'm worried sick and trying to call you). And
I know you don't like swearing, but I'm fucking pissed,
and by the way, I still have my migraine, in case you're
won – [the message cut off there].

What Sarah probably had meant to say, and would have, if she hadn't been a little bit out of it, and if Kevin had come back, is that she didn't really spend a lot of time thinking about her past, or women, or men for that matter. She was attracted to Kevin, she wanted Kevin, she wasn't looking for anyone else.

Because their flight was leaving so early Friday morning, they'd dropped the girls off Thursday afternoon at Kevin's parents, about a half-hour outside of the city. After packing for the trip, they ordered a pizza, and had a date night in. Even the one night seemed like a vacation, with only themselves to think about. They'd fooled around in the living room, and then went in the bedroom, and for the first time in as long as Sarah could remember they'd both fallen asleep after, still naked, with the door open – not worrying about the girls needing anything, being decently dressed to go to the bathroom, or any potential vague emergency they needed to be prepared for. Sarah had woken up a few hours later and gone to the kitchen to get a drink of water. She walked through the house without a stitch of clothes on and felt exhilarated. Standing with the glass pressed against a panel of the double refrigerator doors, the clinking ice reverberated throughout the house. Then standing totally nude in the center of the kitchen where she usually cooked and fed a teenager and a tween — both competing in their surliness — she drank the whole glass quickly, letting half of it spill down her chest and roll off her breasts. It felt like a transgression and she liked it. But when she got back to bed, she noticed Kevin had pulled on his boxers.

She and Kevin had met shortly after she'd returned home from college. They'd spent some time together for the intervening year, and then she'd gone to graduate school. He visited a time or two and asked what she thought about living back in Nebraska after she finished. She hadn't thought about much of anything really, other than where she could get a job with a library science Masters. She got a job in Lincoln, at a branch library. They got married. When she'd called Tully, who had been her best friend to tell her she was getting married, Tully asked "Why?"

Over dinner that night, burgers and some frozen veggie patties (for Gen and Tully, who only ate fish occasionally), Tully had asked why Sarah disappeared after college. Why and how they all lost touch.

"I didn't disappear," Sarah answered, her appetite ravenous since late afternoon — a mix of marijuana and anger. "I just went home."

It seemed everyone else at their college had been from the east coast. She'd felt like an outlier there from so far away; like the other girl, from one of those western states where people don't pump their own gas. The first time they'd all gone out, she'd sat in the driver's seat for a good five minutes before she realized people pumped their own in New York State. It had been a joke told and retold all the first year, laughed at behind hands, that hick, that girl who didn't even know how to pump gas. When Sarah recounted the story of Tully's reaction to her wedding announcement, Tully just shrugged. "That does sound like me."

Sarah smiled wanly, but remembered then how much it hurt.

"You have to know, that wasn't about you, or Kevin. Not that I knew him or anything – I'm just anti-marriage."

"You were," Monica corrected.

"What?"

"You *were* anti-marriage," She prompted again.

"Oh, right," Tully covered.

"Because you came around, you were my maid of honor," Monica looked back and forth between David and Gen.

"Right, now I can see getting married," Tully looked at Gen. But Gen was looking down. Her plate was untouched; her silverware still neatly aligned next to it. Sarah realized that she hadn't heard Gen's voice since they were in town – she'd been silent all afternoon. "Gen, honey, I mean it. About marriage."

When Gen looked up, it was clear she hadn't been listening. Her eyes were wide, stretched open, as if some invisible apparatus was holding the upper lid apart from the lower. The blood vessels were pink and broken, and a crust had formed in each tear duct. She looked right at Sarah, then bolted to the half bath under the stairs. They heard her vomit, then retch dry for some minutes. Finally, Monica nudged Tully to go check on her.

•

"We're going for a walk," Monica was wearing expensive leggings and low-profile running shoes, her curls caught back in baseball cap. David wore short shorts, the kind Sarah would sometimes tease Kevin about wearing, telling him what nice legs he had, that he should show them off more. Despite the beard, Sarah suspected David had a strong chin, and would look just as good without it. She was glad she was wearing big sunglasses this morning, embarrassed about some of the things she'd said last night, telling Monica that she'd found herself *a nice piece of man meat*, asking them if they were monogamous, complaining about Kevin being 'vanilla' in bed. She shouldn't have smoked so much. But after Tully had come back downstairs, saying Gen was resting, looking drawn herself, they'd all needed to lighten the mood. Although if Kevin had heard David's reply to Sarah's question – that they were 'monogamish' – he would have been very uncomfortable.

"Aren't you worried about ticks?" Sarah asked. She'd bought deep-woods insect repellent, and Deet to spray her clothes. She was surprised they hadn't found any yet, or been hounded by mosquitoes.

"That's why I've got the full-body coverage," Monica replied, referencing her outfit with a two-handed flourish. She wore a windbreaker-style zip top that matched her leggings, and some sort of scarf/wrap accessory that filled in any empty space between her top and her hair. Only her face and her hands were exposed.

"I haven't seen many bugs," David said, squinting off into the trees. "Anything from Kevin?"

"No."

"We can head into town when we get back if you want," he offered, "or head back out into the lake – I want to try fishing."

"OK."

But when Monica got back four hours later, hatless, her hair matted down and sweat streaks making snaked tributaries of dirt down her face, David wasn't with her. Tully had checked on Gen, who didn't feel like getting up, but hadn't said so. She hadn't said any words since yesterday. Tully and Sarah were sitting on the end of the dock, rubbing Gen's salve into their ankles and calves and knees when Monica came running out of the undergrowth and kept running toward them at the end of the dock. It took her a long time to catch her breath. She tried to explain what happened on the walk: David thought he saw something in the woods, another person maybe, moving in the trees. He pointed it out to Monica, but she didn't see anything. He'd stop every so often, turning his head quickly, calling out to the someone. At first, she was frightened – thinking there was someone there. But she never saw what David saw. And he wouldn't believe that she didn't see it, whatever it was.

He got impatient with her, then angry. He started yelling at it, them, whatever he was seeing. He took off, chasing it and left her. She tried to follow him but couldn't keep up. She called for him, but he didn't answer, only the oppressive woods and its dense stands of trees, without even bird song. Monica hoped he'd figure out he lost her and double back. But he didn't. She was headed back to the house, and the woods – the thick blanket of humid air (not even a mosquito or black fly) spooked her.

"It seems we've lost the men," Tully joked weakly, and reached out her hand to Monica who batted it away and dove into the lake, a perfect dive that barely disturbed the water. When she broke the surface, she was crying.

"What's going on?" her face crumbling, miserable, asking the question of no one. Sarah kept her sunglasses firmly in place and looked out across the water. Everything was so quiet. If they didn't talk to each other, or tell stories and laugh in the right places, there were no sounds at all. Tully folded her legs up to her chest and rested her chin on her knees.

"Usually, Gen is really voluble. Monica, you know, wouldn't you say she's a talker? But she's been so quiet here, barely saying a word." Monica treaded water at the end of the dock, her water-weighted running shoes flashing at the end of her legs.

"I'm so tired," Monica said. "I think I'll take a nap. Maybe when I wake up my husband will be back."

"I've been thinking that for two days," Sarah answered, and no one laughed.

"Come with me?"

210

"Why not," Sarah waited in the shallows at the shore, supported Monica up the grassy bank. On the porch, Sarah sat her on the edge and unlaced her shoes, gentling them off her feet. She pulled off the socklets, and rested them next to her sneakers, like she would do with her own children. She helped Monica take off her shirt, sports bra, and leggings, and Monica kicked them into the sand, just like Josie would have done when she was half-angry with the world for no clear reason. She started shivering right away, and Sarah wrapped her arms around her, took her upstairs to the 'honeymoon suite,' so called because it was the only bedroom with a private bathroom. She made the shower as hot as she could and put Monica under the spray, stripped off her own clothes and joined her. They lathered each other's hair, using their finger pads to give soft circling massages on the scalp, then finger-combing from root to ends, using the entire bottle of conditioner. The suds washed forest grime, lake water, and fear sweat away. They emerged new. They crawled into the bed that was Sarah's last night, but the night before that had been Kevin and Sarah's, still bearing traces of her nighttime blood let. That afternoon it was theirs. When they slept, it was the best rest either of them had had since they'd arrived. For Sarah, it was the last time she'd sleep without nightmares for the rest of what would be her life.

•

No one felt like eating that night, so they picked at leftovers in the kitchen, filled glasses and drank a few sips before setting them down and filling another. If it weren't for the way

211

Monica stared out the window looking for her husband, it was like a makeshift version of their dorm common room. Tully couldn't comfort her, because she kept looking toward the stairs, then to the underside of the floorboards, a rough approximation of where the second bedroom was, looking vaguely nauseated. Sarah might have appeared the most normal, but she was wearing some sort of longish night-gown with a lace edge (and that wasn't anything she wore in college). Otherwise, both Tully and Monica were dressed identical to their younger selves: cotton pajama bottoms and tank tops. Tully's tank was probably an extra small because she'd always been lean and small-breasted, but her arms were impressive, with tight biceps from all the yoga she did with Gen. Monica's pajama bottoms were a nov-elty print – candy maybe? Or popcorn buckets? Something fun and fluorescent on a white background, paired with a hot pink ribbed tank top that swelled over her breasts and tucked in at her waist. The sun freckled the tops of her shoulders, and when she walked she tripped from time to time on the cuffs of her pajama bottoms.

Tully checked on Gen, reporting that she hadn't stirred, hadn't spoke, didn't look to have shut her eyes. When Sarah peeked in, there seemed to be some sort of clouded film over her eyes, but her pupils searched the darkened room, and Gen reached out her hand. Sarah gingerly sat on the edge of the bed. Where Gen grasped her hand, pulling her toward her, adding the strength of her other hand, she grew her own set of bruises, matching Tully's. Somehow, in that short span of a day, Gen's fingers had become like claws; Sarah could see tendons, wiry and tensed with greenish veins wrapped around muscle. It must be dehydration. She asked Tully if they could get Gen to drink some water, but her friend shook her head. She refused, Tully said, and described her shutting her mouth and shaking her head furiously side to side. Sarah imagined the way the chords of her neck would stand out. What had been impressive about Gen – her sinewed body and lean muscle – was now stripped of any softness, any grace. "It's like she's shutting down," Tully said, and even in the darkening light, Sarah thought she could make out the beginning evidence of another injury on Tully's jaw. Tully looked surprised and blanched. She held a heel of two-day old bread in her hand and picked at it. Not for the first time, Sarah wondered how much Tully and Gen ate, and how much they exercised. Neither of them appeared to have any fat reserves.

They all agreed they were leaving in the morning, with or without the men.

When they'd exhausted any last shred of hope that David would come loping out of the woods, looking beat, but still himself in his poorly-chosen outfit, maybe his beard full of burrs, they closed the outer door. Tully locked it, spooked. They left all the lights on downstairs. All three, by some unspoken agreement, went to Sarah's room and laid down on top of the covers. They woke to an animal crying.

"That's David," Monica bolted upright, in the middle of the other two.

"It's a coyote, or something," Tully whispered. Sarah didn't know why she was whispering. The coyote's call was plaintive, full of pain, and Sarah understood why some people said they sounded like infants crying.

"I know David's voice – that's David." Whatever it was didn't really have a 'voice,' or at least that wasn't what Sarah would have called it. It was a howl, maybe a wolf? Were there wolves in the Adirondacks? She didn't know. And she didn't know how a human could make that sound anyway. It was guttural, and wet, followed by a high keening. Monica had shimmied her way down to the end of the bed and was looking for her shoes – she'd forgotten she wasn't in her own room, that her shoes were outside where she'd shed them earlier in the day. "Oh fuck it." She made for door. "I'm going out there."

Tully and Sarah were up immediately, racing behind her down the stairs, trying not to fall without any hand rail to steady themselves. They weren't quick enough. Monica was at the door, fumbling with the lock, and out it before either of them could find their shoes, or anything to put on. They called after her, but she ignored them, disappearing quickly into the woods.

Tully turned to look at Sarah, "What just happened?" Sarah was silent, her mouth agape, watching the dark space where Monica had been. They heard the noise again, a deep moan of pain, and it sounded close – just beyond the penumbra of light cast from the inside. They both ran inside and shut the door. Tully checked all the windows. They sat up until first light, at opposite ends of the couch, watching out the window, not speaking, eyes honed on the last place they'd seen Monica's body.

•

Once full light arrived, they knew they needed to go. Tully tried to rouse Gen, but the woman who could do crow, handstand, and pigeon yoga poses was fully inflexible. Even with both of them lifting, her joints wouldn't bend. It was as if all the fluids in her body had hardened; beneath her, the mattress itself seemed to have compressed. Lying there over two days, she could have gained another hundred pounds. There was a Gen-shaped hole in the bed, and the bottom of it was Gen.

Plan B was for Sarah to go into town, find a sheriff's office, and a doctor. Gen needed medical attention, they needed to report the missing, and they needed to get out of there. While Sarah was packing her bag, the phone rang. Both Tully and Sarah froze, as if they'd never heard a phone before. It rang again, and they went storming through the house, following the sound. Tully found it, in a back closet, on the bottom shelf. She answered, breathlessly, "Hello?"

"Yes, I'd like to order some of the birchbark wreaths, and some balsam swags."

"What?"

"I'd like to place an order."

"Um, I think you have the wrong number." The line went quickly dead. Tully looked at Sarah, and then looked at the handset in her hands. The phone was a model from the 70's, a peculiar shade of yellow that had faded to a dirty mustard. She set the handset in the cradle, above a rotary dial. It immediately rang again.

"Hello?"

"I'd like to place an order."

"Did you just call here?"

"Do I have the wrong number? It says on the website
. . ."

"The website? Listen –"

"On the website it says you need 6 months advance for special orders, so . . ."

"You've got the wrong number. Can you get off the line?" Tully hung up.

Before Tully could pick it up to dial 9-1-1, the phone rang again. "Hello?" Tully answered.

"Yeah, this is the right number because it's the one on the website. Now I want to place an order."

"Listen, whoever you are. This isn't a company, it's a house, and," but Sarah depressed the buttons to hang up. Tully smiled at her. But the phone rang again. And again and again. "Asshole." Tully unplugged the phone.

So they stuck with Plan B: Sarah would go into town.

•

Driving Monica and David's Subaru, Sarah took it easy over the pitted track called a driveway. She turned onto the gravel road, hitting washboard and trying to steer out of it. When she finally saw the blue-dark flash of asphalt that was county highway, she felt something inside herself lighten. Maybe she'd felt her migraine for so long that even a little lessening felt good, despite all that had happened, and what she had to try to explain to strangers, what was still waiting to be done. But as she turned onto the two-lane road toward town, she felt something like hope. While she was there, she'd call the girls, and talk to her in-laws, and call Kevin again – he couldn't still be mad at her. He probably

just flew home early, needing a little space. She was thinking about Kevin, about seeing him again, and being home,
where the landscape was so different than here: wide open
with much more sky and always telephone poles like mile
markers to warn a person when they went too far – so that
she didn't see the animal down half in her lane, until she
was almost on it and had to swerve and hit the brakes hard,
the car spinning out. When she came to a full stop, and
checked to make sure there were no other cars coming
either way, she took a deep breath to calm herself. Then
she looked in the rearview mirror.

It had springy curls, and wore brightly-printed pajama
bottoms, and one of its bare feet was twisted toward her
so that she could count each of its toes. Where its stomach
would have been was a cavern of purples and reds, its ropey
insides stretched from the shoulder of the highway and into
the stiff tall grass of the ditch. A crow had been working it
over, and returned on a low glide of glossy feathered wings,
landing on the asphalt, returning to the face.

She knew she couldn't leave her there. She knew she
needed to get help for Tully, for Gen. She backed up slowly,
and put on her hazard lights (although no one would end
up passing by). She said terrible things to the crow, incom-
prehensible things, a gibberish of sorrow and hatred and
snot. She laughed some terrible laughter when she thought
of how horrified Monica would have been by the mess,
the unsanitary scene, the way everything was covered with
germs and gravel and fluids and no way to clean. The body
was lighter than Sarah thought it would be, already missing so much – many of the internal organs, a large part of

the back of the head, fingers cut or chewed off one of the hands. Somehow, and she'll never know how, she put what she could of Monica into the hatchback of her own car and drove into town.

•

At the stop sign, she looked left to the little gas station/ bakery/convenience store, and drove on to the end of the street, to what looked like some kind of official building. She parked in the lot and went up to the glass doors. A sign out front announced the summer reading program, and next to it was a Smokey the Bear cut-out with a warning that fire danger was moderate. A taped paper sign said "Summer hours: 10-2. For emergencies, call Sheriff Townsend at home." There was a phone number below, but so sun-faded it was hard to make out. She turned around and pulled in at the bakery. Maria was working. She looked at Sarah's out-fit – the long cotton nightgown stained a soft pink, with an abstract pattern of saturated blood, bile, and brain matter, and said, "Those are bad woods."

Sarah ended up in the back of the sheriff's car, behind its wire grate. He said he wasn't taking any chances, and she didn't know how to ask what he meant. Maria sat up front with him. She didn't need to tell him anything – not where they were staying, or what happened, he seemed to know. He'd asked her for the keys to her car, and took them from her hands carefully, as if touching her was danger-ous. He didn't tell her to get cleaned up, but when she was waiting in the back of the car, he handed her a stack of wet naps and a plastic bag. She used a few to wipe off her face, not realizing she had blood on her forehead (Monica's), not realizing her ear had been bleeding again, snaking a trail down her hairline.

When they began the long drive into the house, he started talking. "Now, I don't know what we're going to find here, so I'm going to ask you to stay put until I know what we're dealing with."

"OK," Sarah had answered. His quick glance in the rear view made it clear he hadn't been talking to her, but to Maria. But even Sarah was unprepared for what they found. She could see Tully on the roof, sitting in her Tully way, her long thin legs folded up underneath her, and her chin resting on them. She was making the animal sound they'd heard last night. The Sheriff hit the automatic window button, rolling them up tight. In the drive behind them was another car, and behind that an ambulance, and behind that a fire tanker. She didn't know how he'd marshalled everyone so quickly.

Tully was rocking back and forth, her face and arms streaked with blood. Her feet were bare. The roof's incline was steep, and Sarah worried she'd fall off it.

"Sit tight," and this time she knew he was talking to Maria. "And you," he turned and looked at Sarah, "stay quiet."

She watched the men carefully approach Tully from below. After a while, she saw a woman who she thought might be an EMT, or maybe a doctor enter the house, then come back out, shaking her head and signaling to the sheriff. He nodded back. The men kept a careful eye on Tully, and all the time their hands on their holstered guns.

Three men went into the house, and she saw one man's head appear through the upstairs window. She imagined he was trying to talk to Tully. If only they'd let her talk to Tully. Finally, the sheriff got back in the car with a clipboard, a pen, and asked her some questions: *How many of them were there? Who was missing? What about the body in the back of her car? Who's the woman on the roof? What about the dead woman inside?* Sarah startled at the word 'dead.' *How long had they been there?* Only since Friday.

He explained that he would have more questions, but for now, they were going to take her back to town, get her some medical attention. He'd see about the situation out here. The situation. By that, Sarah knew he meant Tully. Tully was part of 'the situation.' Maybe David was too, and Kevin. She'd never gotten the chance call him or the girls when she was in town.

•

Outside the car once again, this time with Maria, the sheriff conferred with his people. "He's got to stop doing this – I told him he can't have people out here anymore."

"He probably needed the money. You know his wife is sick." That was the deputy.

"Well, he could have asked for help.

"He did." That was Maria.

"Look," the sheriff tone implied he wasn't in the mood for this conversation. "We've got those two at the house, probably two more in the woods."

"How do we find them?" the deputy asked, not keen to be there any longer than was necessary.

The sheriff searched the sky, saw a wide circle of buzzards to the south, maybe a mile, mile-and-a-half away. "There's one of them," he said, pointing. "I don't want anyone out here more than six hours at a time."

"Got it," the deputy nodded. He'd been working this rural county for six years, and already had to do clean up here twice. That was two times too many. "What about her?" He indicated the woman in the car – she was shaken, and her granny nightgown covered in blood, but she'd come in for help. A good sign.

"She's still walking and talking, so she might be recoverable."

The sheriff grew up here, had always known about these woods. There local legend went that no one who spent a night in these woods survived or, if they lived, they'd wished that they hadn't. When he was a kid he laughed at these stories, even bragged about camping out here. But he couldn't do that anymore.

If these woods were your property, and you couldn't do anything with the land, wouldn't you feel a need to get a little something for your trouble, maybe some coin from a downstate asshole? Especially if you needed it. Say your wife was sick, and your insurance didn't cover the treatment that could help. You loved her. And you had this beautiful place, but no one would buy it, so it just sat, taking more money out of your empty pocket and your wife just got sicker, while you watched.

"Maria, take her to your mother. That's her best chance."

221

They'd torch the house. That was the only way to ensure they wouldn't be here again. They should have done it the first time, or the time after that – but it's hard to hurt your neighbors, the people you see every day at church, the store, dropping your kids off at the library or school. Maybe your mothers were friends as girls, or your wives took turns bringing each other dinners in some tragedy. You watch out for family first, and in towns this small, neighbors are a kind of family, knowing each other's intimate details generation to generation. The sheriff might have loved the landowner's wife before he did, and now imagined her weak under the blue-light of some always-on television; everyone knew it was only a matter of time. Every little bit maybe helped – even if it was only cash to throw at some last-ditch crackpot therapy that brought only a panacea of hope.

The fire truck was idling, ready to wet down the leaves and litter around the house. No use risking the woods – maybe it could be designated some kind of preserve. Guarantee no more building, no development, no people. Maybe there was a grant or something. There had been that scientist some years ago with his equipment and charts – he said he'd been able to track something called 'infrasound' there. But he never came back.

"And her?" the deputy indicated with his chin the woman atop the house, keening that high-pitched sound that sometimes rang through the woods, and had contributed to the local legends. Something about a witch who steals tongues and uses them as lure for the devil. It was terrible to think of: people cutting out their own tongues.

But it had happened out here before. The dead woman in the upstairs bedroom had a tongue in her hand.

"She's too far gone," the sheriff looked down and spit in the dirt. "You know what to do." He put his hand on the younger man's shoulder, squeezed once to show that he wasn't hard-hearted, but that it was a kindness, putting her out of her misery. Maria nodded her head, whether at the logic of the instruction, or the gesture of compassion, it wasn't clear. "Anything human gets burned or goes in the water. If it even looks human. *Missing persons.*"

•

Driving back to town, Sarah still in the back of the sheriff's car, she fell into something like sleep. It might have been getting away from that place again, or pure exhaustion, or maybe something about Maria's presence, which was soothing in its silence – unlike Gen's over the last day, which had tensed and coiled, absorbent. The light was breaking through the branched shade, the way it does in movies in the final scenes, and Sarah could feel the empty space in her brain where her migraine had thrived over the weekend. Absence of pain has a body of its own, tangible, with weight. After a particularly bad episode, Sarah would imagine a melon baller had scooped out some vital portion of her brain. It didn't hurt anymore, but she could feel the sharp and sometimes ragged edges where the kitchen implement sliced its way through – letting a pocket of air live where once was a focal point of misery. She called it her "once-pain," affectionately.

223

She wasn't thinking any of this though – she'd passed out, and the car moved lightly over the overgrown drive, the gravel, and finally the asphalt and into town. She didn't see the ambulance leave, because there was no one deemed in need of medical help. She didn't see the firemen wet down a small circle around the house and ready for a controlled burn. Nor did she see the deputy take aim and fire, a good clean shot. In that moment the keening stopped. Tully's body tipped and somersaulted forward twice, getting caught up for a moment at the edge – the ragged edge of fascia catching skin. Momentum and gravity did its work, dragging the body over. She was so insubstantial that she barely made a noise landing in the dirt. The deputy carried her back into the house, depositing her awkwardly on the couch – then they lit it, and both Tully and Gen burned inside.

Acknowledgements

Thank you to the editors of *Dream Pop Press, Midnight Oil, and The Bend,* where previous versions of these stories appeared.

Much love to early readers of these stories, chief among them Jen Escher (who delivered "Escher Lectures" as needed), Tom Truesdell (who said I might have a knack for the creepy), Mollie Oblinger (who is now refusing to rent a place in the woods with me), and Jennifer D. Sims, who not only read, but delivered line-edits, corrections, and lovingly pointed out my crutches & clichés (with margin notes like "I cannot abide!").

These stories would never have come to be if it weren't for the opportunity to team-teach horror classes with two colleagues, Justin Ponder and Joe Foy. They shared their shelves of books and movies, knowledge about the uncanny, theory, film analysis, community, and the progressive and reactionary messages embedded in horror as a genre. The work we did together served as a catalyst.

Writing doesn't happen in a vacuum, and I've been inspired by so many others – especially the excellent collections of short stories by women that cross genres, weaving horror and erotica, experimenting with folklore and myth, and providing space for complex characters who are neither heroes nor villains, but simply people caught in the complicated structures of their lives. With additional thanks to Linda Williams and Barbara Creed, who allowed me to use their words to structure this collection.

Thank you as always to Apprentice House, and the team of students and faculty who work to help authors like me share our work with the world. My first email from them called the collection "creepy, haunting, and unapologetically sexy" – I felt so seen.

Author Biography

C. Kubasta was born in a small town, a place where the winter light through bare branches always looks a little spooky. Her previous novels *This Business of the Flesh* (Apprentice House), and *Girling* (Brain Mill) explore small-town life through the interrelationships of complex and flawed protagonists. Her poetry is widely available in a variety of journals, and the poetry collections *Of Covenants* (Whitepoint Press), and *All Beautiful & Useless* (BlazeVox). She lives, writes, and teaches in Wisconsin, where she continues to be fascinated by the subtleties of language, meaning, and the stories we choose to tell, as well as those we don't. Find her at www.ckubasta.com & follow her @CKubastathePoet

Apprentice
House Press
Loyola University Maryland

Apprentice House is the country's only campus-based, student-staffed book publishing company. Directed by professors and industry professionals, it is a nonprofit activity of the Communication Department at Loyola University Maryland.

Using state-of-the-art technology and an experiential learning model of education, Apprentice House publishes books in untraditional ways. This dual responsibility as publishers and educators creates an unprecedented collaborative environment among faculty and students, while teaching tomorrow's editors, designers, and marketers.

Outside of class, progress on book projects is carried forth by the AH Book Publishing Club, a co-curricular campus organization supported by Loyola University Maryland's Office of Student Activities.

Eclectic and provocative, Apprentice House titles intend to entertain as well as spark dialogue on a variety of topics. Financial contributions to sustain the press's work are welcomed. Contributions are tax deductible to the fullest extent allowed by the IRS.

To learn more about Apprentice House books or to obtain submission guidelines, please visit www.apprenticehouse.com.

Apprentice House
Communication Department
Loyola University Maryland
4501 N. Charles Street
Baltimore, MD 21210
Ph: 410-617-5265
info@apprenticehouse.com
www.apprenticehouse.com